Praise for the LARRY series

PRAISE FOR The Gospel According to Larry

An ALA Best Book for Young Adults
A New York Public Library Best Book for the Teen Age
A Bank Street College of Education Best Children's Book
A Notable Trade Book in the Field of Social Studies
A *Booklist* Editors' Choice

★ "Tashjian does something very fresh here, which will hit teens at a visceral level. . . . The book's frank discussion about topics paramount to kids—celebrity worship, consumerism, and the way multinational corporations shape our lives—is immediate, insightful, and made even more vivid because it's wrapped in the mystery of Larry."
—*BOOKLIST*, STARRED REVIEW

★ "Tashjian fabricates a cleverly constructed scenario and expertly carries it out to the bittersweet end." —*THE HORN BOOK*, STARRED REVIEW

★ "Tashjian's gift for portraying bright adolescents with insight and humor reaches near perfection here. . . . A terrific read with a credible and lovable main character." —*SCHOOL LIBRARY JOURNAL*, STARRED REVIEW

★ "Tashjian's inventive story is a thrilling read, fast-paced with much fast food for thought about our consumer-oriented pop culture. . . . Teenagers will eat this one up." —*KIRKUS REVIEWS*, STARRED REVIEW

"Tashjian skillfully uses humor and provides one of the most honest voices in young adult literature." —*VOYA*

LARRY
and the meaning
OF LIFE

janet tashjian

SQUARE
FISH

Henry Holt and Company
New York

For Jake

SQUARE FISH

An Imprint of Macmillan
175 Fifth Avenue
New York, NY 10010
macteenbooks.com

Square Fish and the Square Fish logo are trademarks of Macmillan and
are used by Henry Holt and Company under license from Macmillan.

Square Fish books may be purchased for business or promotional use. For information on
bulk purchases, please contact the Macmillan Corporate and Premium Sales Department at
(800) 221-7945 x5442 or by e-mail at specialmarkets@macmillan.com.

Art credits: p. 46, Thoreau's survey courtesy of Concord Free Public Library; p. 63,
photograph of Gandhi © Getty Images; p. 114, illustration of kidney transplant by Birgitta
Sif Jonsdottir; p. 134, photograph of land mine © Wendell Phillips/Adopt-A-Minefield;
all other photographs and illustrations by Janet Tashjian.

Library of Congress Cataloging-in-Publication Data
Tashjian, Janet.
Larry and the meaning of life / Janet Tashjian.
     p.   cm.
Summary: Larry (otherwise known as Josh) is in the doldrums, but after
meeting a spiritual guru at Walden Pond who convinces him to join
his study group, he starts to question his grasp of reality.
ISBN 978-1-250-05035-9 (paperback) / ISBN 978-1-4668-2288-7 (e-book)
[1. Identity—Fiction. 2. Political activists—Fiction. 3. Walden Woods (Mass.)—Fiction.
4. Thoreau, Henry David, 1817–1862—Fiction.] I. Title.
PZ7.T211135Lar 2008 [Fic]—dc22   2007046936

Originally published in the United States by
Christy Ottaviano Books/Henry Holt and Company
First Square Fish Edition: 2014
Square Fish logo designed by Filomena Tuosto

1 3 5 7 9 10 8 6 4 2

AR: 5.4 / LEXILE: 760L

A Note to the Reader

"Breathe," the yoga instructor said. "Really feel the stretch."

I closed my eyes and rotated deeper into the spinal twist. Why had I signed up for hot yoga at my age? Through a torturous exhalation, I thought I caught a glimpse of someone familiar in the back of the room. *Impossible. What's he doing here?* As I switched to my left side, I searched the last row of the yoga studio but couldn't see the face of the teenager in the blue shirt.

"Take a few moments to rest in child's pose," the instructor said.

I stayed in the spinal twist and waited for the kid in the T-shirt to turn around. When he did, I couldn't help but gasp.

"Be careful," the instructor said. "Don't push yourself too hard."

I didn't bother explaining my outburst had nothing to do with sore muscles. I unfolded my legs and faced the front of the room but not before I caught the boy's grin. What did Josh want from me this time?

When class ended, I filled my water bottle and waited for the inevitable. The lobby cleared out, but Josh was nowhere to be found. I hung around a bit longer, then headed to my car.

"I figured since we had our first real conversation in a parking lot, I'd wait for you out here," he said.

Josh's appearances always meant more work for me, but there was no denying I enjoyed seeing him. I asked him what he'd been up to since I saw him last.

"It's a long story." He bent down and reached into his bag.

"No!" I said. "Absolutely not."

"What's your problem?" He held up a water bottle and took a long swig.

"I'm sorry. I thought it was going to be—"

"One of these?" He reached into his bag again but this time pulled out a manuscript.

"You stood up my editor," I said. "There's no way I can help you get that published now."

"I'll make you a deal. Read first, then decide."

"I'll tell you the same thing I told you last time—you're too old for me to write about now."

"What are you talking about? I'm eighteen, same as last time."

I was too tired and sore to argue with his logic and instead skimmed through the manuscript with its footnotes and neatly typed pages.

"Aw, come on. Admit you want to see what I've been up to."

I read the front of his T-shirt. SUNDAY, MONDAY, TUES-DAY, WEDNESDAY, THURSDAY, FRIDAY, SATURDAY. SEE—NO SUCH THING AS SOMEDAY. More out of curiosity, I stuck the manuscript into my bag. Josh strapped on his helmet and unlocked his bike.

"How can I get in touch with you?" I asked.

"I'll get in touch with you," he answered. He cruised down the road with his arm in the air, flashing me a good-bye peace sign.

I walked to the adjacent café and ordered a large coffee. Josh Swensen—he ran a popular anticonsumerism Web site until he faked his own death to escape the flood of pub-licity. Went into hiding, then emerged to run for president at age eighteen. After that, he'd taken off cross-country to find his girlfriend, Janine. I knew a bit about his recent escapades but was curious to know more. As I sipped my coffee and began to read, I already knew I'd end up help-ing him. He was like a second son to me, someone who wanted more than anything to change the world.

How do you say no to a kid like that?

Janet Tashjian

LARRY

and the meaning

OF LIFE

Larry and the Meaning of Life —
in my own words
by
Josh Swensen

PART ONE

"Things do not change; *we* change."

Henry David Thoreau
Walden

There is nothing good on television at three o'clock in the morning. I've spent months doing research; I know. Like a media-fueled zombie, I clicked from channel 02 to 378 then back again, night after night. The programming was dreck, but the images and sounds comforted me. I'd been home for a few months after traveling the country by bus to try and find my girlfriend, Janine.[1] After eight months on the road, I realized she was history. When I returned home, my stepfather, Peter, gladly removed his treadmill from my old bedroom. My best friend, Beth, was less than an hour away at school—I should've been happy. But this was the most miserable period in my life.

Peter tried not to let me see his growing concern. He slapped me on the back and told me I just needed time to settle in. He threw the stack of woe-is-me letters I'd written from the road into the fireplace, setting off a handful of sparks.

---

[1] A quirky girl I'd met in Boulder, Colorado. She never gave me a reason to doubt her, yet I blamed her for the information leak in my presidential campaign. I should've realized betagold—a meddling, upscale senior citizen who outed my Internet identity and stalked me for years—was behind it. One of the biggest mistakes I ever made was believing Janine had betrayed me.

"All kids go through this," he said. "Being rudderless at your age is the most normal thing in the world."

"That's the first time anyone's ever used the *n*-word to describe me."

"See? There's hope for you yet."

I turned toward the fire, avoiding eye contact during yet another humiliating personal conversation. "I hate to sound like a walking cliché, but I don't know why I'm here. I don't know what I'm supposed to be doing with my life."

"Have you tried talking to your mother?"

I told him last time I tried she wasn't there.[2]

"Nonsense. Probably just a bad day. But maybe this will help. Beth's father called—there's a part-time job at the hardware store if you want it."

I'd already bungled my September start date at Princeton and was scheduled to begin classes in January instead. I knew I needed to work between now and then, but I'd replaced the requisite job search with *South Park* reruns. Rerun—I was only eighteen, yet my whole life already seemed like one.

"The hardware store sounds great. I'll call him tomorrow." As much as I'd always enjoyed filling the bins with bolts and mixing paint colors, the thought of getting up, showering, and being at the store by 7 A.M. sent me burrowing deeper into the cushions of the couch.

---

[2] My mother died several years ago, but I cooked up a great way for us to talk. I hang around her favorite makeup counter at Bloomingdale's, ask her questions, then wait for people to walk by with the answers. Up until last year, my system worked perfectly. I tried to tell myself the communication technology was just being updated, not that she'd deserted me forever.

"Once you get to school, you'll be fine. You're always happiest when you've got a project to keep you busy."

"I tried to change the world and failed," I said. "Several times. Just making it through the day is about all I can handle right now."

"I think it's time to talk to a professional."

"A truckload of Prozac couldn't help me deal with how messed up the world is."

"Is that what's bothering you?" Peter asked. "The state of the world?"

"There's conflict on every continent, the poverty rate is increasing, the environment's a wreck, and I'm not supposed to be affected?"

"Maybe you should get involved in solutions instead of sitting on the couch complaining." The touch of anger in his voice reminded me of the old Peter, the workaholic ad exec who'd married my mom.

"I did that, remember? Got my head handed to me on a platter. Spent months writing sermons, spearheading a grassroots campaign for change—nothing."

"You've been through a lot," Peter said. "You're just exhausted."

"I feel like I'm sleepwalking and I'll never wake up."

"I've got to admit I'm worried," he said. "I've never seen you like this." Peter sat with me awhile before going to bed.

It wasn't that long ago my life felt full of purpose.[3] Maybe

---

[3] The purpose might have been twisted, like breaking into the principal's office and downloading the theme from *Jaws* onto his MP3 player for the school awards assembly, but at least there *was* a purpose.

Peter was right and this was just a blip on the radar screen, a phase that would end once I entered college. But when I really stopped to analyze it, losing the election or the state of the world wasn't the problem—I was. Being so directionless was new territory for me. I'd always prided myself on knowing what I wanted to do: fight consumerism, run for president, change the world. I'd filled notebooks and blogs with ideas and projects since I could remember. Now? I'd tried to write a few sermons since I'd been home but came up dry. Watching an episode of *Family Guy* seemed much easier to manage. And since I stopped hearing my mother's voice at Bloomingdale's, I felt more lost than ever. Talking with her—alive as well as dead—had been a beacon for me, a way of continuing to improve myself and grow. My biological father had died before I was born; for some reason lately, that early loss throbbed like a new wound. If he were alive, would things be different? Peter—at least this recent, caring version—was helpful and kind, but even he couldn't jumpstart my malaise.

When I started the www.thegospelaccordingtolarry.com Web site, some people had called me a guru, but I was the first person to say the term never applied to me. Those long months on the road made me realize I didn't have any answers. And as much as I looked forward to college, it seemed naive to think some professor would take me under his or her wing as a spiritual protégé.

I picked up the remote and clicked—infomercials, Nick at Nite, *The Terminator*. I sank deeper into the couch, hating myself for choosing the wonderful world of distractions over the difficult job of fixing my life.

"I can't believe you bagged my father," Beth said. "You *love* the hardware store."

"I know—I can't get out of my own way."

"Getting out of your way implies movement. You haven't left the couch in months!"

While studying at Brown this semester, Beth had let a local hairdresser chop and highlight her hair, which was now as short as I'd ever seen it. Surprisingly, the severe style actually softened her expression, tempering the razor-sharp ambition that was usually the first thing you noticed about her. "I can't keep taking the train up from Providence to talk you off the ledge."

"Especially when the ledge is a *Twilight Zone* marathon," I said.

Beth grabbed the remote from my hand and shut off the TV. "Come on, let's go to the woods. Sitting in your hole for a few hours always makes you happy."[4]

I answered her by getting up and turning on the TV by hand.

---

[4] Years ago, it took me a month of afternoons and Saturdays to dig the ten-by-twelve-foot space. It was the setting for many a vision quest and night of solitude—not to mention the place where Beth and I finally hooked up last year.

She shut it off and blocked my path. "This is all because of Janine, isn't it?"

"No."

"Are you sure?"

"Positive."

"Why don't you start a new blog and write a few sermons? You'll feel better."

I told her I'd tried but the words wouldn't come.

"One word in front of the other, like laying bricks," she suggested.

"It's a bigger problem than just writing sermons. It's life in general."

Beth rolled her eyes with exaggeration. "An existential crisis, how unique. You're eighteen, a little too young to give up on life, especially without having lived most of it. You know how much stimulation you need—you're just bored."

I ran through the many projects I'd accomplished since I'd been home: a collage of found objects from the Radio Shack Dumpster entitled *Technical Difficulties*; helping a neighborhood family run a yard sale to benefit Guatemalan refugees; hacking into the town library's computer system to order several books on astronomy; organizing Peter's books into chronological, alphabetical, categorical order; perfecting a new chocolate dessert; and applying for a patent for my acorn energy processing system.

"And you still have time to sit around and mope?" Beth asked.

"My projects usually motivate me, but now they just feel like fillers to take up time." I lifted the hem of her jeans, exposing her antimaterialism tattoo.

She swatted my hand away and threw me my jacket. "I'm taking out the big guns. We're going to Walden."

I covered myself with the jacket and curled into a fetal position. "I feel like I've let down Thoreau. I can't face him."

She yanked the jacket off me. "Stop being such a baby. He's been dead for a century and a half. I doubt he's worried about your productivity."

I didn't want to admit I'd avoided Walden Pond since I'd been home. Being in a state of mental and emotional disarray at such a sacred spot only added to the torque of my downward spiral.

When Beth forced me to look at her, the expression on her face showed only tenderness and concern. "I'm worried about you."

"You sound like Peter."

"He's worried too."

"You two talked about me?"

"He doesn't know how to help you. Neither do I."

"I'll tell you what you both can do—leave me alone."

She looked at me for a good long time. "On one condition. You at least *try* to help yourself."

"Okay. I'll go to Walden tomorrow. Happy?"

Like the best friend she is, Beth volunteered to come with me. As much as I would've enjoyed her company, I told her I wanted to experience the pond in solitude. Maybe Henry David could provide some much-needed solace. The thought cheered me up momentarily, until a second one followed right behind it: two of the biggest influences to guide me on life's journey were dead.

13

I had to admit it was great to be back at Walden. My body leaned into the earth, relieved to once again be supported by its fertile arms. Watching the orange maple leaves descend to the surface of the pond made me realize there was no other place I'd rather be.

From my favorite spot, I gathered a small pile of acorns and tossed them into the water.[5] I rolled up my jacket, propped it underneath my head, then stretched out on the lush soil. "*Simplify, simplify*," Henry David Thoreau had written after spending two years, two months, and two days in this sacred place. Year after year, I kept returning to his words. The advice seemed ridiculously easy, yet in practice proved immensely difficult. Minimizing my number of possessions wasn't a problem—I still logged in at fewer than seventy-five—but reducing the number of distracting thoughts that continually derailed me was next to impossible. I closed my eyes and let the word form a cerebral loop: *simplify, simplify, simplify, simplify, simplify, simplify. . . .*

------

[5] Why was I the only person besides squirrels to think of using them as an energy source?

I was jolted out of my meditation by a middle-aged man with wild gray hair, wearing a dirty Hawaiian shirt and overalls with one side of the denim bib unbuttoned. He stood above me laughing.

"Thinking about Henry David or dreaming about a warm grilled cheese sandwich?"

I told him I'd been thinking about Thoreau.[6]

"All the pilgrims come up here, thinking that if they stare into the green water long enough, their lives will change." He took a knife and small piece of wood from his pocket and began to whittle.

"Is that a rook?"

He held up the small object. "Chess is a great game—a lot like life."

I lay back down on my jacket pillow. "I'd hardly call life a game."

"That's where you're wrong. There are goals, other players, and instructions laid out before you start."

"That's funny, I don't remember reading the inside cover of the box before being born."

"Just 'cuz you don't remember reading the instructions doesn't mean you didn't."

Who *was* this guy?

As if in response, he held out his hand. "Gus Muldarian. Come here every day to walk the pond."

---

[6] I hadn't felt hungry but could hear my stomach growl after he mentioned the grilled cheese sandwich.

I introduced myself and told him I loved to walk around the pond too.

He unfastened the other button of his overalls. "No, I said what I meant. I walk the pond." He took off his overalls, revealing a patchwork pair of denim cutoffs. His chest and abs seemed as strong as the foundation of a building.

"Be careful, the pond gets deep," I warned.

He took an elastic from the jumble of bands on his wrist and tied back his long hair. "Thoreau himself was the first person to survey the pond—winter of 1846, while it was still iced over—using a compass, chain, and sounding line." He pointed across to the other shore. "The deepest point is over there—a hundred and two feet. I walk as far as I can, but where it's over my head, I tread."

He marched to the shore repeating the sentence like a singsong poem: *Where it's over my head, I tread. Where it's over my head, I tread.* I spent the next hour staring up at the canopy of trees but found myself continually drawn to the water to see if I could spot Gus. He reminded me of some of the wacky travelers I'd met on the road. I couldn't tell if he was Latino, Middle Eastern, Native American, or just plain tan from the remnants of summer. I'd been coming to the pond for years but had never seen him before. My overactive curiosity got the better of me as I stared at his overalls and shirt strewn on the ground. You can tell a lot about a person by what he does—or doesn't—have in his pockets. I made sure he was on the other side of the pond before rifling through his stuff.[7] I unfolded a

---

[7] It's a bad habit, I know.

16

stained piece of notebook paper and stared at the words scribbled across the page in pencil. Memories flooded in of being stalked several years ago by betagold. I put the paper back in his shirt, grabbed my jacket, and sprinted up the hill. The words haunted me as I ran toward the road. *Josh Swensen.*

Walden Pond

"I'm sure there's a reasonable explanation why some stranger had your name in his pocket," Beth said. "He's probably doing a where-are-they-now piece for his blog."

From a logical point of view, this made sense. But something in my gut screamed to the rest of my body to pack my bag and hit the road.

Beth's expression was a unique combination of wanting to comfort her best friend and urging him to get over himself. She was the one person on the planet who could always cut my self-absorption to the quick. She ripped open the netting of a small crate of clementines on the counter and tossed me a fruit. I took this as a sign to move on and steered the conversation to her political science class, a course I'd audited a few times since I'd been home. But halfway through our discussion of the electoral college[8] my mind veered back to the wild man at the pond.

"Don't you think it's creepy being stalked by some aging hippie spouting Thoreau? Who knows what he wants?"

_____

[8] Don't get me started. See my book *Vote for Larry* for my views on *that* can of worms.

"This is so you," Beth said. "Instead of asking the guy face to face, you take off and spend the next days obsessing about it. If you want me to go with you and find the guy, I will, but we are *not* spending the next few weeks playing 'What if?'"

I couldn't admit I'd already gone back to the pond looking for Gus Muldarian with no luck. First Janine, now Gus—I could never make a living as a private detective. In the usual way she could read my mind, Beth asked about Janine. I told her I still hadn't received an e-mail or call.

"What about that guy from your Soc class?" I asked. "Does he still want to go out with you?"

Beth told me he was more extinct than the spectacled cormorant. She stopped peeling her clementine and pointed to the space between us. "You're not thinking about us as a couple again, are you? Any chance we had evaporated when you took off after Janine."

This was what I loved[9] about Beth. She always gave you exactly what was on her mind, both barrels.

"I was just asking," I said. "Don't flatter yourself." I went back to making a tabletop mosaic of a *Simpsons* couch scene with the tiny pieces of clementine peel.[10]

Beth took pieces of peel from her own pile and added them to Marge's hair. "I mean, it makes sense logistically for us to hook up again with both of us around, not seeing other people."

---

[9] Yet hated.

[10] The spongy white stuff inside citrus rinds is called albedo. I beat a guy at Scrabble in a cyber café in Phoenix with that one.

"On the other hand, there's nothing wrong with waiting," I said. "Sometimes that's the best plan."

As nonchalantly as possible, I checked out Beth's ironclad expression. I'd known her so long and would guarantee she'd rather be with no one than be someone's second choice. Nights I couldn't sleep, I wondered if choosing Janine over Beth had been the wrong decision. I made a choice, but it didn't work out. Life goes on, right?

Peter came in and threw his baseball cap onto the coatrack across the room. He'd parlayed his stint as my presidential campaign manager into a full-time job as an events planner for several grassroots candidates. I still couldn't get used to the beard and the jeans, a look miles away from the corporate robot uniform he'd worn during his marriage to my mother.

"Josh, I need you to write one of your speeches for this local candidate I'm working with."

For what seemed like the millionth time, I told him I was out of the sermon/speech/rant writing business.

"This guy's a carpenter by trade—got into politics to fight the zoning laws. Hates those giant McMansions as much as you do. Come on, it'll take you two seconds."

There were people who did this for a living, and I told him I was no longer one of them.

"Come on, give it a try for your old man."

His perkiness made me realize there was no local candidate, that the whole thing was a ploy to get me to focus on my work again. Peter's manufactured enthusiasm sunk my already low self-esteem even lower. Almost as if he realized what I was thinking, Peter backed off and handed me a small box that had come in the mail. No return address, just my name in a handwritten scrawl. Inside was a rook with a note. *Still think life isn't a game? Your move.*

The note was unsigned, but I knew who'd sent it. I threw the note away as if it were radioactive. The feelings racing through me reminded me of when betagold—aka Tracy Hawthorne—ruined my life.[11] Was Gus the 2.0 version? Why couldn't people just leave me alone?

Beth was right; I needed to confront Gus and put an end to this before it got out of hand.

---

[11] The first time.

I'd spent hours—make that years—mulling over my character flaws. First off, my attention span was scattered at best; I continually zigged and zagged through endless lists of ideas, some of them implemented, many of them not. I found it difficult to be in social situations for too long.[12] But the trait I never seemed to be able to improve upon was how difficult it was for me to let people see the "real" Josh. I expended an enormous amount of effort hiding behind screen names, bumper stickers, and secret identities with no luck. I was Josh Swensen,[13] end of story. I still cringe when I think about hiding the real me from Beth on my Web site. Whenever we're on the cusp of an argument, Beth continues to remind me of that particular transgression.[14]

As I biked down Route 2, I gave myself a reluctant pep talk. *Face this guy like a man. Find out what he's up to. Let him see you're not afraid.*

---

[12] Make that *large* social situations. I could have an in-depth conversation with someone at a bus stop but high school? It gave me the creeps.

[13] Or was I Larry? Even I didn't know anymore.

[14] *The Gospel According to Larry* illustrates this weakness.

But I *was* afraid. I'd been run over by political mobsters, framed as an embezzler, even attended my own funeral—all I wanted for the next few months was to sit in my hole and do nothing. The last thing I needed was a washed-up celebrity stalker stalking a washed-up celebrity like me.

I locked my bike in the parking lot and headed down the hill to the pond. After a few moments I spotted Gus wading along the shoreline. I had to give the guy credit—the water was sixty degrees, tops. Hoping the cool water would bolster my efforts, I pulled my jacket and shirt over my head, kicked off my sneakers, and waded in. The water's temperature was jolting, but its clarity was even more of a shock. I could see my jeans, my feet, and several trout swimming by.[15] As I closed the space between the mysterious stranger and me, I found myself inexplicably grinning. This was the most alive I'd felt in months.

"Awakens the mind, doesn't it?"

I'd been careful not to let Gus see me enter the pond, and I'd made as little noise as possible. It was as if the guy had eyes in the back of his head.

"In the winter, I walk *on* the water instead of in it." The acoustics of the pond carried his chuckle back toward me. "Walk on water, I like that."

I jogged toward him until I finally caught up. We faced off like two busts in an aquatic art installation: *Two Heads in Historic Pond Discussing Nothing Historic.* I imagined a miniature

---

[15] The pond is an oligotrophic kettle hole, which means not a lot of organic nutrients grow there. Between that and the ban on outboard motors, the water is exceptionally clean.

cartoon version of Beth hovering over my shoulder whispering encouragement in my ear. *Don't let him off the hook. Find out what the hell he wants. Tell him to leave you alone or else.*[16]

"Who are you?" I asked. "And how'd you get my name and address?"

Gus's expression showed not only mischief but kindness. "Is that what scared you off the other day? You were *meant* to find that paper in my pocket. There are no accidents—you should know that by now."

I ignored the imaginary Beth on my shoulder; this guy was intriguing. As we treaded in silence, I spotted the two giant koi that lived in the pond.[17]

"Buddhists often release fish as part of their hojo-e ceremony," Gus said. "They're very big on life being liberated."

"Who isn't?"

"We need to liberate your mind. That's why you'll meet me here every day, rain or shine. We'll discuss the rules of life, and you'll perform the tasks necessary to achieve enlightenment."

"Enlightenment? I can barely figure out how to get through the day."

"Exactly. That's why you need a guru."

"A *guru*?"

"Call it what you want—guru, teacher, mentor. No one makes spiritual progress without one."

"I was just thinking about having a mentor the other day."

---

[16] Beth's encouragement usually resembles a tirade more than a pep talk, but it's what I've come to expect from her.

[17] There used to be three, but I hadn't seen the third one in years.

"Of course you were."

He dove into the pond and came up holding a small trout. I'd spent enough time by the water to know how nearly impossible it was to catch a fish with your bare hands. He closed his eyes and held the fish for a moment before throwing it back in. "Enough questions for one day. We have more important things to do—namely, to walk."

Every time I said the word *but* Gus held his finger to his lips to silence me. I finally gave up and treaded toward the far end of the pond. Truth be told, I was tired of being stuck, tired of wallowing in my own screwed-up-ness. Even if he was a bona fide wack job, what did I have to lose?[18] By the time I reached my clothes, I decided I wanted to study with Gus. I envisioned the cartoon mini Beth, hands on hips, shaking her head in disbelief.

---

[18] Don't answer that.

After spending the morning with Gus, I felt like I'd known him for years. No, I felt he knew *me*. Better than Janine, Peter, or even Beth. Better than every other person in my life except one.

I hadn't been to Bloomingdale's since I'd returned to Massachusetts and could feel the anxiety buzzing through my organs like electricity.[19] Since I was here last, they moved the store to the mall across the street. I wandered around the new location until I found Marlene, my mother's favorite salesperson, holding court behind the center counter.

"Joshie! Come over here and give me a kiss—come!" She gestured furiously for a hug, and I obliged.[20] "Where have you been? I haven't seen you in ages."

---

[19] Did you know there's enough electricity in our brains to run a fifteen-watt bulb? Unfortunately, Mr. Nardone didn't appreciate my experiment in sixth grade with a refrigerator bulb, electrodes, and a borrowed Red Sox cap. I don't care what sports fans say, I still take credit for breaking the curse that led the Sox to finally win the World Series years later.

[20] She was the only person on earth I'd allow to call me Joshie—that's how much I liked Marlene.

I filled her in on my cross-country trip, then told her the last time I was here, my mother didn't speak to me.

"She's been here plenty of times since—even I've heard her." Marlene sat me down on the stool and pretended to show me an anti-aging serum.

I knew Marlene hadn't conversed with my mother since her death, but I appreciated the vote of support. Marlene had aged, but her penciled-in eyebrows, bowl haircut, and giant glasses still made her seem like the crazy aunt I'd always wished I'd had.

Marlene ducked behind the counter to make a quick phone call. I didn't want to get her in trouble, so I pretended to examine the products in front of me. As I scanned the list of ingredients, I realized I was stalling, not to protect Marlene but myself. What if Mom was truly gone? The permanence of life without our "conversations" reverberated inside me again. Mom was the most alive person I'd ever known[21] but her zest for life made her death that much more painful. She'd packed a lifetime's worth of laughing, dancing, hiccuping, swimming, cooking, and making up stories into her short time on earth. Even standing in front of thousands of screaming supporters on the campaign trail paled in comparison to how much fun it was to carve a pumpkin or sit on a park bench with her.[22] Since her death, my biggest struggle had been to force myself to view the world in its true

---

[21] Until she died, of course.

[22] She used to call it telekinetic picnicking. We'd sit in the park with enormous concentration and try to trip people as they walked by. She could make even the most stable pedestrian tumble over a blade of grass, I swear.

vibrant colors, not the monochromatic version it appeared to be when I woke up each morning and realized she was still gone.

Marlene cruised by with a customer and whispered, "Joshie, she's here today. I know she is!"

I got off the stool and shuffled toward the escalator. "Mom? Are you listening? Can you hear me? I need to talk to you."

I stood in the aisle and listened. Nothing.

A woman walked by entering text into her BlackBerry. Another stopped at the counter beside me and picked up several lipsticks before heading to the shoe department.

Somebody say something—anything!

A man with a blue suit and matching cell phone walked toward me. The Bloomingdale's makeup department was the only place I was actually glad to see a cell phone; it meant someone would be bringing my mother's words to me. But this customer was listening, not talking. No use to me at all.

"Mom, I've found someone who wants to be my spiritual teacher. Is he a crackpot or authentic? I need you to talk to me—come on."

Two high school girls in plaid uniforms bounced from display to display ogling the new autumn shades.

"I think he's for real," the first girl said.

The other girl rummaged through various testers. "I'm not so sure."

"You met him for a reason," the first girl said. "I say go for it."

"Yes!" I pumped my fist into the air, scaring the girls to the next counter. The reception was so good, I half expected my mother to glide down the escalator in full heavenly splendor. Instead, a harried woman in expensive sweats tugged her

29

toddler off the moving stairs with such force the little girl burst into tears and dropped her aardvark plush.

I crouched down and returned the toy with a whisper. "Trust me, when she's gone, you'll even miss days like this."

The woman thanked me for the doll and jostled her daughter toward the exit.

"Did you hear your mom?" Marlene asked.

"Loud and clear," I answered.

"See?" She handed me a small gift bag of samples and told me to give them to Beth.

I stood in the middle of the department one more time. Was it greedy to ask for one more encounter with my mother?

A blond woman with three inches of black roots passed by talking on her cell. "Oh, once isn't enough? You know what you need to do, now do it!"

So, so, so my mom.

I avoided Beth's phone calls and biked to Walden the next day. It took two walks around the pond before I found Gus. He was at the site of Thoreau's cabin, sitting atop the cairn.[23]

"I'm not sure you should be sitting up there," I said. "It's kind of sacred, don't you think?"

Gus stood up and beat his chest like King Kong. "I think *should* is the first word we should ax from your vocabulary."

I didn't tell him he'd just used the word himself.

"So, you decided to enlist," Gus said.

"You make it sound like the army."

"Spiritual boot camp—you're exactly right."

"Muldarian . . . what kind of name is that?"

"Armenian." He jumped off the makeshift memorial with unexpected grace for a man his size. "Let's go meet the others."

I couldn't hide my surprise. "Others? I thought you were the guru and I was the student."

"You think you're important enough to warrant one-on-one attention?"

---

[23] A spontaneous memorial made of stones. If you capitalize it and add an *s*, it's a city in Australia.

"It's not that," I said. "I just thought—"

"Another bad habit we should break you out of."

This time I couldn't help myself. "You said *should* again."

He wrapped his arm around me and pulled me toward him in a bear hug. "*Now* you're paying attention."

We walked toward the small beach at the south end of the pond. He finally released me from his grip when the path became too narrow and we were forced to walk single file.[24] Although it was October, several people sunned themselves on shore. A few people my age sat on the stone wall dangling their legs in the water. Both women had hair down to their waists and wore jeans and hoodies. The three guys all had a few days of chin stubble that was meant to look casual but actually took days to get just right.[25] Their identical dress shot a warning directly to my gut.

"This is Josh," Gus told them. "He'll be joining our group."

"Hi, Josh," they said in unison.

I suddenly wondered if Gus was recruiting for Alcoholics Anonymous. I gave a quick wave then looked down to my feet. Was I making a giant mistake?

The others paid rapt attention as Gus spoke about the importance of commitment to a spiritual path. I tried to stay focused but felt distracted by the bait and switch. If Gus was running a camp for Spiritual Wanderers, why didn't he say so?

---

[24] I wonder what Henry David would make of the wire fence and the AREA CLOSED TO THE PUBLIC—PLEASE KEEP OUT signs surrounding the pond now. I realize they're protecting an ecosystem from half a million visitors a year, but it still seems so un-Thoreau.

[25] Believe me, I've tried. It takes forever.

When Gus discussed the group's daily routine, the five other "students" raced for their notebooks. I rummaged through my pack but found only a pen. I took notes on the palm of my hand until one of the girls in the group handed me some paper. The whole thing was beginning to feel like junior high—in a word, humiliating. I figured if I made it till noon, I could fabricate some excuse and hightail it back home.[26]

Gus sensed my lack of enthusiasm. "Josh obviously has more important things to do. Why don't you share your thoughts with the rest of us?"

Junior high, nothing—make that fourth grade. I decided to cut short my losses. "No offense, but this isn't for me. I misunderstood your program. I'm sorry."

Gus didn't look a bit annoyed as he continued to wade through the pond. "You thought you were someone special who deserved a teacher all to himself."

"It's not that."

"You think you're better than these other pilgrims, more evolved."

"No, of course not."

"We've got another group of disciples coming today. Kids like you from all over the country looking for meaning in their lives." Gus opened his arms wide to encircle the panorama of the pond. "I'll tell you what I think. You're the most lost soul here. I think you came out of the gate quickly with lots of purpose, then floundered. An eighteen-year-old burnout, that's what you are. You used to have ideas on how to change the

---

[26] *Three Stooges* marathon, here I come.

33

world, how to save the planet, but now you can't figure out how to save yourself."

It's as if he was living in my frontal lobe. Gus went on for several minutes—about how I had a lot to learn from these other "disciples," how my morbid self-absorption would only lead to more despair. How I needed to wake up to the world around me. Parts of his rant actually reminded me of some of my own. Still, the regimen he laid out seemed like a lot of—what's the word?—oh, yeah, work.

I returned the paper to the girl next to me and got up to leave. I wished them all luck, Gus included.

"You make your own luck," Gus said.

"I'd love to stay and bandy around more clichés, but I've got to go."

"Don't get carpal tunnel from using that remote!" Gus waved goodbye with no trace of animosity.

As I walked up the hill to the parking lot, a group of kids my age was heading to the pond. They wore the same jeans and hooded sweatshirts as the students back at the beach. As I passed through the group, I studied their faces. It was only a fleeting glance, but I had to admit they seemed happy and serene.

It wasn't the girl in the back that got my attention; it was the dog trotting along beside her. The collie suddenly ran toward me and jumped up, placing his front paws on my chest. The dog's tail wagged furiously as he licked my face.

The girl stood beside us laughing. "Looks like Brady missed you."

I gently let the collie down and grabbed Janine.

34

Where had she been living? What was she doing? I fired questions at Janine, but she insisted on attending Gus's lecture. I didn't want Gus to think I'd changed my mind about his program because an old girlfriend showed up, so I biked around Concord for the rest of the morning and met Janine back at Walden for lunch. She looked amazing. Her waist-length hair was a hundred-and-eighty-degree change from Beth's cropped do. It took a while to get used to Janine in these clothes; her zany sense of style was one of the things I'd always loved about her. She smelled like oranges, and her skin was tan and smooth. I asked if she'd continued her habit of silent Mondays[27] and if she still went to concerts all the time.[28] After the small talk, I told her how I'd traveled across the country to find her. Turns out she'd been in L.A. studying with Gus.

"I went to Gus's first lecture on a lark. Guaranteed enlightenment—I mean, come on." Janine fed a bite of her hummus wrap to Brady. "But I started noticing these amazing changes in my life. I've been following him ever since."

---

[27] She didn't.
[28] She did.

I asked her what kind of changes.

"I feel as if my life has a purpose now, you know what I mean?"

"Unfortunately not. The word *purpose* has jettisoned itself from my internal dictionary."

"You of all people," she said. "That's a shame."

Somehow admitting I'd lost a grip on something so important seemed a huge concession to make, even to Janine. Truth was, I found her new assuredness unnerving. It sounded petty, but of the two of us, I'd always been the one with a clear game plan and she more or less tagged along. I can't say I appreciated our psychic switcheroo.

"Who are all these 'students'? Are they runaways?"

"Of course not!" she laughed. "A lot of them are taking time off after high school. Some study with Gus part time. It's totally voluntary—he's legit."

"I guess it can't do any harm to listen in."

She put her hand on mine with what seemed like platonic support. "It's always a good idea to follow your heart."

Great—more clichés. But I told her I *had* followed my heart, six thousand miles' worth. "It's not your fault—no one had a gun to my head to find you. But between that and losing the election, the meaninglessness crept in, pulled up a chair, and made itself at home."

"I'm sure you'll turn it around. I have complete faith in you."

Her happiness *had* to be fake. I decided to test her newfound tranquility. "Beth's doing great at Brown. Political Science, Drama Club. I see her all the time."

Janine seemed ecstatic. "I'm so happy for her."

36

"She looks stunning. Short hair, fit. Really hot."

"She was always so beautiful."

This was not working out as I'd expected.

"Maybe I will sign up to study with Gus. Maybe Beth and I *both* will."

Janine beamed. "That sounds like a terrific idea."

I couldn't even look at her; my small-mindedness was embarrassing even to me. I'd spent lots of time with Janine when we lived in Boulder, and she'd never had this quiet composure. I looked back down the hill to Gus and his students. The "guru" was skimming stones into the pond with such ease, I half expected him to retrieve the rocks by walking on water, even with the pond not frozen. He was right about one thing: I may have dashed out of the purpose gate at an early age, but the rest of the world wasn't waiting for me to catch up. The few months I'd spent wallowing around at home suddenly seemed like chains I needed to break free of.

I've never been the club-joining type,[29] but maybe it was time to start.

---

[29] "I don't care to belong to any club that will have me as a member" (Groucho Marx).

"Sounds like a cult," Peter said. "And a guru named Gus?[30] Please!"

Beth agreed. "Gurus aren't supposed to be stalkers. You don't even know who this guy is. He could be some con artist trying to scam you out of your life savings."

"I have fewer than seventy-five possessions. I hardly think anyone's going to get rich off me."

"At least let me check this guy out, make some inquiries," Peter said.

I told him I didn't care who the guy was—he'd done wonders for Janine.

"I'm glad she's doing well," Beth said. "But that doesn't mean this program will work for you."

"Hear, hear," Peter agreed.

Beth stopped the glider we were both rocking on. "How did she look, by the way?"

"Janine? Great."

---

[30] The name Gus held fond memories for me. The only other Gus I knew was our old mailman, who'd lent me his uniform to escape the press camped outside my front door a few years ago. I didn't tell Peter I counted this memory in the plus column of the pros and cons list I'd put together regarding studying with the new Gus.

She nodded and started up the glider again. "Skinny?"

I shrugged. "I guess so."

"Good skinny, though, right? Not too skinny, I hope."

I told her Janine looked good.

" 'Cuz sometimes you can get *too* skinny."[31]

"I wasn't focused on her weight," I answered. "She just seemed content."

"Sure it's not drugs?" Peter asked. "You can never tell with these cults."

"It's not a cult. I'll be living *here*! I can leave anytime."

"Is her hair still long?" Beth picked at her tiny bangs. "It's not like I care, I'm just wondering."

"You're so focused on the externals, maybe *you* should take a course in spiritual enlightenment."

"I'm not the one playing D & D in my basement all day."

"As of tomorrow, neither am I."[32]

"Please don't do this," Beth said. "And I'm not saying it because Janine will be there."

"My mother said Gus was for real."

"No offense, but I wouldn't make a life decision based on people standing at the Chanel counter," Peter said.

"It's always been my most important decision-making criterion—you know this!"

---

[31] I obviously don't have a lot of experience with girls, but does this nonsense ever end?

[32] As long as I could find a way for a small party of high-level adventurers to permanently destroy the Tarrasque from the 3.5 version rules by using obscure magical items and a finely tuned spell list, which I'm making based on every rule book, campaign setting, and magazine dealing with version 3.5.

Peter mumbled something about learning from my own mistakes, then lit the grill for dinner. I waited until Beth left before I dropped the bomb I'd been saving since yesterday.

"Uhm, there's a fee to study with Gus," I said. "Two thousand dollars."

Peter turned the knob of the grill with so much force a stripe of orange flame leaped toward his head. He jumped back and lowered the burner.

"Two thousand dollars? Whatever happened to 'all you need is love'?"

I explained that lots of teachers charged tuition, including those at Princeton. *He* explained he'd been working almost pro bono since he left his advertising job and barely had any savings left.

"Never mind," I said. "I'll make other arrangements. Don't worry about it."

Peter turned off the grill; it seemed neither of us were hungry anymore. I headed to the basement.

Since I was a kid, the back-and-forth movement of the cellar swing had served as a mental metronome for me. After climbing on, it took only a few moments for the repetitive motion to calm my mind.

I had to admit that Beth and Peter weren't the only ones with doubts. Suppose Gus further derailed my already-precarious mental state? And I couldn't say I was looking forward to being in "class" again. The longer I thought about it, the more reasons I came up with to bail on the whole thing. But a little sliver of hope deep inside forced its way to my consciousness. *You're sick of just lying around. You want your life to have meaning again. You need help getting out of your own way.*

I remembered a quote from Joseph Campbell that I'd read in tenth grade: "I don't believe people are looking for the meaning of life as much as they are looking for the experience of being alive." The quotation summed up my feelings exactly. I didn't care about the why of life so much as I just wanted to partake in it again—with full attention and participation. I didn't want to sleepwalk anymore; I wanted to be awake. I just had to find a way to make it happen.

Peter came downstairs and sat cross-legged on the floor next to me. He pushed me on the swing as if I were a toddler at the playground. I was embarrassed by his fatherly attempt at connection and braked the swing with my leg.

"If you really want to do it, I'll lend you the money," he said. "It's up to you."

I thanked him for his generous offer and told him I'd repay him in full.

"You're right about that," Peter said. "With interest."

"No way," Gus said. "You wanted out, you're out. I'm not taking you back as a student because of an ex-girlfriend.[33] What do you think this is—two years ago, when you ran that anti-consumer Web site to impress the girl next door?"[34]

I explained that Janine recommended his program highly and that was good enough for me. Gus listened for several moments without speaking.

"You'll have to prove yourself," he said. "If these other kids give one hundred percent, you give two. If I'm setting up a utopian community, I can't have kids waffling back and forth on their commitment." Gus whittled a knight from a piece of maple as he spoke.

"Whoa! Utopian community—are you talking about a commune?"

"Did I say commune?" Gus asked. "I'm talking about a community of people who live together with common goals."

---

[33] Gus didn't know, but I'd already done exactly that. Impressing Beth was one of the reasons I'd kept up the initial Larry Web site in the first place.

[34] Scratch that last footnote.

"That's the definition of a commune."

"Well, I found a three-story Victorian down the road, a Victorian Utopia. Think I'll call it Victopia."[35] Gus beat his hands on his chest and let out a Tarzan yell. "The other students will stay there, but I think you should commute. You're much more the commuting type."[36]

When I held out the check for two thousand dollars, Gus snapped it up faster than a tree frog snaps up flies. "Welcome to Utopia, my boy. Whatever's in your internal world will manifest itself in the outside world. Make sure what you bring to the group is positive."

He shook my hand and told me to get ready to work my butt off.

I spotted Janine down by the water. She and several other students were walking the circumference of the pond from the inside, the way Gus had done that first day.[37] I walked to the shoreline and yanked off my sweatshirt. I stumbled to

---

[35] Massachusetts was actually home to two of the first utopian communities in the country. Fruitlands was started by Bronson Alcott in the 1840s; his daughter, Louisa May, wrote about their experiences there after she published *Little Women*. Another progressive thinker, George Ripley, started Brook Farm in West Roxbury in 1841 with Thoreau as an early supporter. Both communities were founded with the best intentions by the brightest minds, yet both failed. I'd learned these interesting facts while pretending to be the substitute American History teacher for three days junior year.

[36] What does *that* mean?

[37] Does the tuition cover wet suits?

the water until I reached Janine. "I want to feel alive again. I'm in."

She ran her hand along the surface of the water and splashed me in the chest. I dove in and popped back with a frigid scream. Up at the treeline, I spotted Gus watching us through a pair of high-tech binoculars. He was several yards away, but I could swear he was laughing.

PART TWO

"Man is firmly convinced that he is awake;
in reality he is caught in a net of sleep and dreams
which he has unconsciously woven himself."

Gustav Meyrink

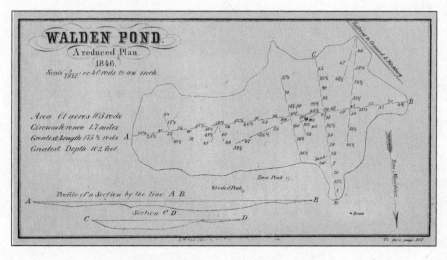

An engraving of Thoreau's 1846 survey
from the first edition of *Walden*

I'd be lying if I said personal enlightenment was the only thing on my mind after finally seeing Janine again. It had been a while, and we had a lot of time to make up for. Until Gus set the group's ground rules.

"Rule number one: There'll be no chatting up the opposite sex," he said. "You're here for one reason and one reason only—to focus on your studies. Celibacy is a given."

What?

The smirk on his face made me think he had Janine and me in mind with this first rule. But, unlike me, Janine seemed to gladly accept the regulation. I forced myself to suck it up and pay attention to the rest of Gus's lecture.

"Rule number two: Possessions tie you down. For those of you new to the group, it's time to get rid of your belongings." Gus passed a stained pillowcase around the circle, and we tossed in our gear.[38] MP3 players, cell phones, books, and

---

[38] With only a few possessions to my name, this was easier for me than for some of the others. When Katie got rid of her designer bag, she looked as if she was saying goodbye to her best friend.

makeup, as well as IOUs for the possessions we had at home and would bring in the next day.

"Your auras look lighter already," Gus said. "Rule number three: 'Idle hands are the devil's workshop.'"[39] Gus handed out photocopies for us to share. They appeared to be hand-drawn maps of the pond and its surrounding areas. "As you may know, Thoreau was a man of many interests—writer, naturalist, philosopher, gardener, house helper for Ralph Waldo Emerson. But of all his skills, surveying was a way for him to support himself and tramp through the woods at the same time."

I studied the tiny numbers measuring the pond in rods,[40] taking special pleasure in Thoreau's messy handwriting, as difficult to read as my own.

Gus pulled a well-worn paperback of *Walden* from his back pocket. "From chapter sixteen. 'As I was desirous to recover the long lost bottom of Walden Pond, I surveyed it carefully, before the ice broke up, early in '46, with compass and chain and sounding line.' Back in Thoreau's day, some people thought this glacial hole had no bottom, that it was so deep it went right through the center of the earth. Thoreau proved them wrong with a cod line and stone." It seemed as if Gus was looking straight through me. "Sometimes we get so lost, it feels as if we'll never reach the bottom of ourselves, but like finding the floor of Walden, all it takes is some good, hard work."

I watched the water lap to the shore, afraid to look Gus in the eyes. Was I the only one whose insides felt like a bottomless

---

[39] Can I make a case for using Rule #3 as a reason to get rid of Rule #1?
[40] One rod equals sixteen and a half feet.

abyss? I hoped I wasn't the most screwed-up person in the group.

"Thoreau performed more than a hundred fifty surveys in his lifetime but only a few here at Walden," Gus continued. "We're going to take up where he left off, learning this skill and surveying the rest of the area."[41]

Mike was first to complain. He was a big guy from Kansas City, who'd joined the group after his sister claimed studying with Gus had changed her life. "Haven't other people surveyed it since Thoreau? Why do we have to do it again?"

Gus explained the exercise wasn't busywork but would force us to follow in Thoreau's footsteps, metaphorically, as well as physically. He opened a box filled with several rusty artifacts. "These are from the same time period as Thoreau, so please be careful."

We sorted through the plumb lines, angles, compasses, and weights. I don't know how the others felt, but I could sense the history embedded in the antique metal, linen, and wood. Gus split us into groups for the survey work. Mike was assigned to work with Janine and me. The three of us hiked to the west end of the pond.

With all the walking and meticulous measuring, it didn't take long to break into a sweat. "And to think we had to pay to come here," I said.

---

[41] Thirteen years before Thoreau calculated the measurements at Walden, another soon-to-be American icon was making a living surveying in Illinois— Abraham Lincoln.

Mike stopped counting his steps. "You had to *pay*?"

I stopped counting also. "Didn't you?"

He shook his head and asked how much studying with Gus had set me back. I was too embarrassed to tell him my step-father had to underwrite my spiritual journey, but Mike nagged until I relented. I mumbled the words "two thousand dollars" as we started back on our task.

"Are you insane?" Mike pointed to the others farther up the hill. "None of them had to pay. You can never trust those Lebanese."

"Armenians," I corrected.

I looked to Janine for support, but she told me to take it up with Gus. After finishing our first assignment, I did. He listened while I raised my grievance, putting down his whittling to give me his full attention. When I finished, he thanked me for sharing my feelings, then picked up his wood.

"That's it?" I asked. "Thanks for sharing?"

"Sharing is not something to be taken lightly," he answered. "It's a very sacred activity."

"I agree. I'm just wondering why I had to pay such an exorbitant amount when no one else had to."

"Maybe you should stop worrying so much about other people," he said.

"And everyone else gets to live in that big house down the road while I bike in every day. It just doesn't seem fair."

"Who said life was fair? That's a concept guaranteed to bring unhappiness."

Intellectually I knew he was right, but that didn't stop me

from obsessing about the inequality of Gus's program for the rest of the day. The downward spiral I'd been experiencing these past few months seemed ready to envelop me for good. It took all my willpower to resist it, forcing my mind to focus on the surveying instead. Like Thoreau, I was determined to reach the long-lost bottom.

After spending four hours surveying,[42] we settled in for Gus's lecture.

"I had a talk with a student earlier today about fairness, so today we'll discuss an ethical dilemma dealing with questions of life and death, fairness and responsibility."

He closed his eyes for several minutes and basked in the autumn sun. This guy definitely knew how to build suspense.

"Suppose a man needed an organ transplant," Gus began. "A man, like all of us, who'd been sometimes good, sometimes bad, but had repented. Suppose he had a rare blood type, but you were a match. Would you consider donating a piece of your liver, your kidney, your lung?"

"Why go through all that hassle for a stranger?" Mike asked.

"Because the man will be dead by the end of the week if he doesn't have the operation. Because only two percent of the population is a biological match. Because you're young and healthy and would probably weather the operation with few

---

[42] I loved surveying for the same reason Thoreau probably did—a job walking outside and observing nature? Sign me up. I'd already surveyed more tracts than the other students combined.

complications." Gus closed his eyes again and garnered the sun to his face like a solar panel. "Would you do it *then*?"

Vigorous discussion ensued regarding the risks and benefits. We talked about the common good versus individual needs. In the end, most of us agreed to help save a stranger's life.

"Good," Gus said. "Now let's add another factor. Suppose this person who needs the transplant is in prison."

Katie asked him to clarify.[43]

"He's a murderer doing a life sentence. Or maybe he's on death row, waiting to be executed."

Why save a murderer? Why donate an organ to someone scheduled to die? Aren't there worthier people who could use our help? Gus might've been playing devil's advocate, but he couldn't understand how the new details were relevant. "There is no us and them.[44] In an enlightened life, there's only we."

"I wouldn't let myself get cut open for a murderer," Mike said. "Absolutely no way."

I took the other side of the debate. "Convict or not, he'd still be dying. If he could live another thirty years with some bone marrow I wouldn't miss, why not?"

"So your bone marrow could rot in prison?" Mike asked.

"Who knows? Maybe while he was in there, he'd find a cure for Alzheimer's or design a new hybrid engine."

---

[43] Even without her cell, Katie's fingers constantly typed a phantom keypad. I'd never seen such a serious case of texting withdrawal.

[44] As long as we get to keep the Pink Floyd song.

"Or kill someone else," Mike said.

I could tell from the look in Janine's eyes she knew why I'd taken this side of the argument. She knew I'd watched the life slowly seep from my mother's body; being able to help someone delay that inevitable decline would be worth any temporary and personal inconvenience.

"Can we talk about something else?" Janine asked with a slight stutter. "This discussion is totally hypothetical."

"It doesn't have to be," Gus said. "I've done volunteer work at the National Kidney Foundation, one of the many organizations that facilitates living organ donation." He reached into his pack and took out a pair of rubber gloves, some gauze, and a box of syringes. "This is completely voluntary, but a simple blood test can determine if any of us would be viable donors to the long list of people waiting for transplants. I can't think of a better way to put a theory of changing the world into practice."

"Not for a murderer, I hope," Katie said.

Gus tied the tubing around his arm, then held it taut between his teeth.[45] After letting go of the tubing, he told Katie the list was full of deserving recipients, not convicts. Up the hill, the train heading west punctuated our collective silence. Given the stand I'd taken in the argument, I didn't have much ground for backing out. I rolled up my sweatshirt and held up my arm. I'd given blood many times since my mother's illness; another sample was no big deal. Mike mouthed the

---

[45] With a little too much intravenous expertise, if you ask me.

word *brownnoser* as Gus stuck the needle into my arm.[46] Janine went next. She appeared upbeat, but I could tell her bravado was a facade. Everyone except Mike gave samples.

Gus held up the vials, now filled with deep red blood. "We can discuss these ethical dilemmas for days, but this is a whole new level in commitment to finding out the truth—*your* truth." He told us he had to package the samples for the lab, and we should finish the day's surveying.

"A girl I know from high school has been waiting for a tissue transplant for months, but I never thought of volunteering my own," Katie said later. "I'm a perfect example of Gus's theory—talking about making the world a better place but not doing anything about it. I'm going to see what blood type she is and see if I'm a match."

"Gus isn't going to do anything with those samples," Mike said. "It's all for show. He is one crazy Albanian."

"I thought he was Armenian," I said.

"He told me he was from Pakistan." Katie pointed toward Janine. "Ask her—she's his favorite."

The conversation devolved into an am-not, are-too harangue between Katie and Janine.

"We're here for spiritual enlightenment, not one-upmanship," I said. "Knock it off."

"You could've stood up for me back there," Janine told me later. "Katie hates me because Gus let me keep my cell."

---

[46] I think it's safe to say I was the first person to ever have a phlebotomy experience on the shores of Walden Pond.

"How'd you get to keep it?"

She shrugged and smiled mischievously. "I guess he just likes me."

I put my arm around her. "So why don't you get him to relax the celibacy rule too?"

"Very funny." She ducked out from my arm and threw a stick to Brady. Park rules forbid pets, but Janine insisted on taking him there every day anyway. Surprisingly, she hadn't been caught.

We walked away from the water toward the tracks. While he lived here, Thoreau never thought of the train as disturbing his peace and quiet but embraced the noise as part of his surroundings. "Did you know the railroad company built an amusement park here after Thoreau died?" I asked. "There was dancing, football fields, even a racetrack."

"Thoreau probably would've hated it."

"His sister Sophia thought it was profane." I took the stick from Brady's mouth and threw it again. "What else were you doing in L.A. besides studying with Gus?"

"Nannying, surfing, waitressing—the usual Southern California thing."

I focused on Brady running up the hill to avoid looking at Janine when I asked if she'd thought about me while she was gone.

"Of course I did. But I'll tell you what I didn't miss—feeling I'd let you down." She suddenly screamed Brady's name.

When I looked up, I saw that Brady had wandered toward the tracks. I raced after Janine, who grabbed him by the collar moments ahead of an oncoming train. She knelt down and buried her face in his fur. I took a mental photo of what I admired most about Janine—the way she didn't care who was looking when she demonstrated her love. I was in awe of the way her heart ruled her life. Her mind didn't analyze the world at a hundred miles per hour the way mine did. She was uncomplicated and beautiful, and I'd let her get away. Earning back her trust might prove to be even more difficult than completing Gus's program.

"Today we're studying another leader in the nonviolence movement, a man who read Thoreau's 'Civil Disobedience,' put its principles into practice, and changed the course of history." Gus spent the next hour talking about Mahatma Gandhi and the nonviolent revolution that led to India freeing itself from British rule. He talked about Gandhi's Salt March—a 248-mile walk to harvest salt from the sea.[47]

"The locals were forced to buy cloth from the British, so Gandhi decided they should make their own. His wife taught him how to use her spinning wheel—he spun his own cotton until the day he died. He considered the spinning wheel an outward symbol of truth and nonviolence."

I wondered if Gus would pull a mini spinning wheel from his pack and teach us how to use it. What he pulled from his bag was even worse.

"We're not going to spin," he said. "We're going to paint." He took out several boxes of the paint-by-numbers kits I'd used as

---

[47] The British levied heavy taxes on salt; Gandhi's idea was that people gather their own salt from the sea, bypassing the tax and denying Britain the revenue, as well as asserting the independence of Indian citizens.

a kid.[48] "I want you to practice the same focus and care with these as Gandhi did spinning cotton."

"Spinning cotton served a purpose," I said. "The locals could make their own clothes." I held up a paint kit of a cheetah in the forest. "How is painting this useful? Who am I defying?"[49]

"Gandhi said, 'One hour spent in spinning should be an hour of self-development for the spinner.' *That's* why you're doing it."

A flicker of movement in the brush caught my eye. When I went to check it out, I found a man with a videocamera. He stammered something about trying to find the cabin site; I told him it was farther up the hill. He seemed embarrassed and hurried by us.

"We need to focus through distractions," Gus said. "Let's go."

We passed the paint kits around, each of us more perplexed than the next. The illustrations of the finished products seemed old-fashioned and kitschy, hardly worth hours of our time. Yet Gus beamed like a parent on Christmas morning watching his children open their presents. He told us to get cracking.

"This sucks," Katie said under her breath. "I really feel like sitting here on a sunny day and painting a stupid clown."

Mike motioned toward me. "Larry is paying for the privilege."[50]

I told him to shut up and opened my box. Inside were seven tiny pots of paint and a canvas divided into sections of numerical

---

[48] My mother never let me use the kits as given. She'd switch the numbers on the lids of each tub of paint so every canvas I did came out psychedelic or just plain bad.

[49] Besides people with artistic taste.

[50] I told everyone, including Gus, to call me Josh, but they all insisted on calling me Larry.

and alphabetical space. I made mental formulas with the numbers as I wiped the thin brush on my sweatshirt and broke open the first color. When Gus finally told us to put our paints away, I was shocked to discover an hour had gone by. The enormous concentration I'd used to paint the geese formation kept my usual barrage of thoughts at bay.

Gus stood behind me and admired my work. "Like meditation, right? Only with your hands."

I had to agree.

"Wait till you see what we're going to do with these. I expect your very best work."

I didn't need Gus's encouragement. As soon as I got home, I set up the canvas on the kitchen table. I knew better than to take Beth's phone call, knew better still not to tell her about my new project, but I did both anyway.

"A paint-by-numbers epiphany? Talk about mindless conformity. What's next, how to achieve nirvana by hooking up a DVD player?"

I told her not to knock it until she'd tried it.

"And why waste your time surveying the pond? I'm sure you can find the same maps at the town hall."

"The Concord Library, actually. But I'd hardly call emulating Thoreau and Gandhi a waste of time."

"No offense, but it's like talking to your mom at Bloomingdale's. Kind of random, don't you think?"

"Life *is* random—that's the point!" I answered.

"Is embracing the randomness the point? If that's it, maybe you're done."

"I've got to go. You're distracting me."

"Remember the private investigator from Denver I used to track you down?[51] Why don't you give her a call and ask her to check out Gus?"

I told Beth I'd committed to following Gus's path and wasn't interested in any tawdry tidbits some P.I. might dig up.

"But what if innocent kids are getting screwed out of their life savings?"

I intentionally forgot to tell Beth I was apparently the only student who'd paid tuition.

"Can I just give you her name?" she asked. "Please?"

I wrote down the investigator's information as a way of finally getting off the phone. But after I finished painting the last goose, I found myself staring at the piece of paper on the counter. What if Gus *was* running some kind of cult? What if Janine was wrong and some of the students *were* runaways? I decided a simple phone call couldn't do any harm.

The investigator remembered Beth. "She was determined to find you. I had a lot of fun tracking you down at UC."

I took my incognito-ness[52] as a compliment, then asked about doing a basic background check on someone. I also told her I didn't have a dime to my name.

"Don't worry about money yet," she said. "If this new guy is half as much fun to check out as you were, I'd do it for the sport."[53]

---

[51] After I dropped out, Beth wouldn't let it go and hired someone to find me hiding out in Boulder. See *Vote for Larry* for a more detailed explanation.

[52] Don't bother looking it up; it's not a real word.

[53] Yeah, right.

I gave her Gus's basic information; she said she was going on vacation and would give me a call when she returned. She seemed nice enough, but I couldn't fight back the creepy feelings inside. Was I being cautious or betraying my new teacher? Should I judge Gus on his present actions or past? Suppose the guy's background was sparkling clean—would I feel relieved or untrustworthy for going behind his back? I chose to work through the ethical dilemma by breaking open another tub of paint.

Gandhi and his spinning wheel

I couldn't decide which activity I liked more—taking meticulous notes as I studied the land or dipping the thin brush into the acrylic paint. Say what you will about Gus, but both activities calmed my overactive mind even better than the basement swing. I loved the silent focus and amassed stacks of survey maps and paintings. At our afternoon meeting, Gus motioned for one of the canvases. I handed him the clipper ships.

He held the small canvas in the center of our circle. "Very good work here. Nice attention to detail."

I was glad Gus appreciated my efforts. Then he took a Zippo lighter from the pocket of his overalls. I watched in alarm as he lit the corner of the painting on fire.

"What are you doing?" I asked.

"Practicing impermanence and nonattachment. You're learning a valuable lesson."

"I worked hard on that one.[54] And what about Gandhi? He believed in impermanence, but his work served a purpose."

"Didn't this painting perform a service? Didn't it focus your mind?"

_____

[54] Why hadn't I given him the one with the napping kittens instead?

I muttered yes but told him it still seemed wasteful.

"What's wasteful is to hold on to things after their usefulness is gone." He turned to the group. "Like your MP3 players and your phones. You let them go. Now you're free."

He dropped the remains of the canvas onto the sand and told me I was one step closer to enlightenment. "Even though you'll all be saying goodbye to the finished product, I want you to take enormous care, understand?"

We agreed.

Gus popped a raw garlic clove into his mouth then pulled out a crumpled piece of paper from the pocket of his overalls. "Moving on. The donor organization I contacted ran through our blood tests and found two of us matched the criteria for someone on their list."

"I still think it's crazy to give a cell of my body to a murderer,"[55] Mike said.

"Let's not get into that ethical can of worms again," Janine added.

"You won't have to," Gus said. "The person on their list is hardly a criminal—she volunteers in a homeless shelter, teaches Sunday school, and builds houses with Habitat for Humanity. She's been waiting for a kidney for over a year, and two people are a match—Janine and Larry."

Katie and the others looked visibly relieved. Janine buried her face into Brady while I wondered why I'd ever gotten off the couch.

"You're both eighteen, you don't need parental approval,"

---

[55] A cell would probably be useless, but I knew what he meant.

Gus said. "But you should discuss it with them anyway. The recipient's insurance pays all medical costs." He popped another garlic clove. "I'm not attached to this idea—if anyone can think of a better way to do something besides talk about making the world a better place, I'm all for it."

As the others packed up for the day, I stared at the charred remains of my painting. When people talked about letting go, were they referring to artwork and body parts? Would helping a worthy individual with a serious medical problem be the jump start I needed to stop overfocusing on my own life and plug into a greater purpose? Changing the world had been my mantra since I could talk. Helping another person live would be a tangible step on that path. Did I have the courage to do it?

It wasn't Peter who went bananas; it was Beth.

"Are you out of your mind? My uncle donated a kidney to one of his buddies from Desert Storm and he's been in and out of the hospital ever since! And for a stranger? I can't believe you're even thinking about it."

"Don't get your thong in a twist—thinking is all I'm doing."

"After all we've been through together, you expect me to believe you've only been thinking? No, Josh, you've already visited every Web site dealing with organ donation, haven't you?"

"No comment." I reached into the pockets of my Salvation Army pea coat and took out the two bags of microwave popcorn I'd brought to accompany our midnight viewing of *Monty Python's Life of Brian*.[56] "Young, healthy people like me go on to lead totally normal lives."

"Well, that would be a first." She unscrewed a brown lipstick from the bag of samples from Marlene.

Please try it on. Please.

---

[56] I didn't rent *Monty Python's The Meaning of Life*—the organ donation scene with Graham Chapman removing the liver from an unwilling and very alive donor hit a little too close to home.

"If you think giving away one of your organs is some short-cut to solving your existential crisis, you're wrong."

"Have I ever told you that I *hate* how well you know me?"

"Would you rather I just agree with your latest idea, no matter how off the wall?"

"Basically, yes." Why did I pick the most obstinate, rational person on the planet as my best friend?

She stood next to the microwave listening for the corn to pop. "What did Peter say?"

"He was against it until I brought up my mother. An organ donation wouldn't have helped with the cancer, but suppose she had a different disease? Imagine if she could've lived because someone donated an organ. Wouldn't you want someone to donate an organ then?"

Beth dumped the popcorn into the striped plastic bowl we'd been using since sixth grade. "I hadn't thought about it that way." She handed me the bowl and asked what Janine was going to do.

"She was pretty woozy after the blood sample. I can't imagine her making it through the necessary tests. But she told Gus she wanted to move forward. I'm not sure if she's doing it to help the recipient or get on Gus's good side."

Beth's cell vibrated across the table.

"Your phone hasn't stopped all night," I said. "Is that your new Brown boyfriend?" I shoved a handful of popcorn into my mouth to downplay the question.

She buried her cell into the sofa cushion. "I'm in four different study groups at school. The pressure is ridiculous."

"Then how come you're home so much this semester?"[57]

"My dad needs help at the store. A certain friend of mine bagged him, remember?"

"I'd help you tomorrow, but Gus wants Janine and me to meet with the donor organization."

"Oh, if it's Gus's idea, you should definitely do it."

Beth's voice wasn't dripping with sarcasm; it was flooded with it. But she had a point. Was I thinking about getting cut open to generously help another or as some kind of desperate exorcism? Was I unnecessarily risking my life to avoid feeling so dead? These were the questions that worried me more than life with only one kidney.

On the way to Walden the next morning, I stopped by the local woods to hang out in my hole. Peter had heard several acres had been sold to developers, and sure enough, a back-hoe and port-o-john now graced the large tract of land. Soon there would be new holes, much larger than mine, lined with concrete and transformed into family rec rooms. I imagined the large rectangular spaces filled with Ping-Pong tables and exercise equipment. My own den—half a mile in—seemed tiny in comparison. I sat inside for several hours trying to analyze the pros and cons of donating an organ to someone in need. Gus was right about one thing—for someone interested in personal growth, being forced to make such a choice was the ultimate talking the talk.

When I finally got to Walden, I chained my bike to the rack.

---

[57] It's because of me, right? Just admit it.

As I approached the replica of Thoreau's cabin,[58] I heard giggling. Gus and Janine sat inside the tiny building on the reproduction of Thoreau's cot. He had his arm around her. Janine jumped up when she saw me, but Gus remained seated.

"Looks like you expelled a lot of toxins on your ride." Gus motioned toward my sweaty shirt. "Perfect day for it."

Janine kept herself busy by picking at the mattress. I asked if we could talk.

"If it's about the organ donation, your ex here beat you to it," Gus said.

"You already said yes?" I asked Janine.

She nodded, but a touch of anxiety infiltrated her peaceful smile.

I pulled her away from the cabin. "Are you doing it because of him?"

"Who?"

"Him!"

"Gus? Of course not. Can't you give me more credit than that?"

Gus took out his whittling gear, ignoring the group of tourists trying to photograph the cabin. With his wild hair and worn overalls, he looked like he could've been part of an old Yankee re-enactment.

I led Janine away from the group. "What was that about back there?"

---

[58] Thoreau built the original cabin himself, spending twenty-eight dollars and twelve and a half cents on materials. Today you could spend that much on a hammer in Beth's dad's hardware store.

70

"What was what?"

"That!" I motioned toward Gus.

"We were just talking. What's your problem?"

I turned to face her. "Is he hitting on you?"

When she told me not to be ridiculous, I told her Gus wouldn't be the first guru to ignore his own celibacy rules to enjoy the company of a female disciple.

"Why are you still studying with him if you think he's a creep?" Janine asked. "You're a hypocrite, and that's worse."

"At least admit he was flirting with you. I'm not an idiot. You're donating your kidney to a stranger to get in good with Gus."

"You're jealous that I'm not your little student anymore, that someone else might be teaching me about the world." She ducked into the women's restroom before I could respond.

As I watched the door close behind her, I wondered about this latest piece of information about our "leader." Was he enlightened or just a dirty old man trying to meet trusting young women? Heading into the men's restroom, I caught a glimpse of Gus across the parking lot. He'd pulled out a chair from the cabin and was leaning back in the sun. For the first time, his eyes and smile seemed impenetrable.

Replica of Thoreau's cabin at Walden Pond

I tried not to obsess about Gus and Janine but found my mind involuntarily going down that sordid track. I'd exercised great control in following Gus's rules of conduct, and it drove me crazy to think Gus might not adhere to the same principles. Of course, there was no evidence to corroborate my new theory; all the betrayal and hypocrisy existed solely in my overactive imagination. Or so I hoped.

Janine asked me to watch Brady while she and Gus ironed out the details of her organ donation downtown. I willed myself to be mature, but Janine saw through the act.

"There's nothing going on with Gus and me. Can you just get over it?"

"How long will you be gone?"

"Probably a few hours. I'm trying to get as many tests done in one day as possible."

I told her I was still ready to take her place as donor.

"Well, if I flunk any of the medical screenings, I'll remind you you said that."[59] She bent down to Brady, but he turned away from her. "I'm worried about him—he hasn't eaten in a

---

[59] Rut-ro.

73

few days. I'm taking him to the vet tomorrow. Just let him tag along with you, okay?"

I led Brady down to the water for a swim, but it was difficult to concentrate on throwing sticks when all I could hear was Janine and Gus's laughter echoing from across the street. After a few minutes, I couldn't take it anymore and guided Brady up the hill toward the cabin site.

I sat on the ground inside the ten-by-fifteen space. I realized I'd unconsciously dug my own hole to similar specifications. With thousands of acres of forest all around him, Henry David hadn't needed larger living quarters. I felt the same way. I leaned back against the chains that marked off the sacred site and rubbed Brady's belly. I barely looked up when someone approached.

"This is a landmark and a state reservation," the voice said. "No dogs allowed—there's a fifty-dollar fine."

"I know," I said. "I tell my friend all the time."

"You know it's not allowed, yet you're doing it anyway?"

"He isn't mine." I stood up and extended my hand to the ranger. "My name's Josh Swensen. I'm here with—"

"You're here with a dog," the ranger interrupted. "Remove the animal from the park now."

I tried to remember who the ranger reminded me of when it dawned on me: Todd, a stupid jock from high school Beth used to date. This ranger seemed even more obtuse than Todd, if that were possible.

"I'm on my bike so I can't take him now. How about if I sit in the parking lot with him till my friend comes back?"

74

The ranger took the walkie-talkie from his belt. "I've got a belligerent tourist at the cabin site," he said.

"I'm not belligerent, and I'm not a tourist. I'm here every day."

"Requesting local backup."

"Are you kidding?" The last thing I wanted to do was get into a feud with this Neanderthal, but his overreaction to the situation made me dig in my heels. "The only way you'd need backup is if Brady here licked you to death."

"Visitor is threatening bodily harm," the ranger said into the walkie-talkie. "Request immediate assistance."

"Are you smoking crack? That was a joke!" Forget donating a kidney; this guy needed a funny bone transplant pronto. My own sense of humor failed to kick in, however, when two local cops slid their way down the hill.

"This is your final warning," the ranger said. "Remove the dog from this site immediately."

Brady's sense of humor was obviously intact, because he chose that exact moment to lift his leg and pee on the stone marker commemorating Thoreau's hearth. Letting out a raucous laugh was probably not the best reaction on my part. The two new officers grabbed my arms and led me up the hill.

"There's no reason to manhandle me," I said. "I'm happy to take the dog out of the park."

"Little late for that." The ranger tried to grab Brady's collar, but the dog wasn't cooperating. He bared his teeth and barked at the ranger. "I don't suppose you have a leash for this monster."

"He's a collie, and he doesn't feel well. You're aggravating

75

him." I told the cop on my right that I'd be happy to grab Brady if he'd remove me from his ironclad grip. When he looked straight ahead without answering, I told him he was being very un–Thoreau-like.

"You, on the other hand, will be very Thoreau-like," he answered. "Spending the night in jail when you didn't have to."

"*What?* That's ridiculous. You're blowing this out of proportion." The first ranger grabbed Brady so hard he yelped. "Knock it off before I start screaming police brutality," I said.

The cop twisted my arm even further as he threw me into the squad car.

"This is Walden Pond! What is your problem?"[60]

The ranger shoved Brady into the back of his van.

"Since the jail where Thoreau spent the night is gone," I suggested, "why don't you just let us off at the top of the road?"

"Lucky for you," the ranger said, "the current police station has a few modern cells for your enjoyment."

I was furious with the overzealous officers but just as angry with Janine for purposefully disregarding the posted laws. I'd call Peter to bail me out of these trumped-up charges, then track down Janine in the city with Gus.

Unfortunately, Peter's, Beth's, and Janine's phones all went to voicemail. I sat in the cell cursing all of them. Then I remembered one of Gus's teachings from earlier in the week: *Life is like photography—you need the negative to develop.* Must be

---

[60] I didn't want to get into even more trouble so I didn't bring up a line Thoreau had written in his journal on February 13, 1860: *Always you have to contend with the stupidity of men.*

76

nice coming up with snappy similes while hanging out in Boston with Janine.

As I stared up at the ceiling, I couldn't help but compare myself to Henry David in this same situation more than a hundred fifty years before. The night he'd spent in jail was a revelation for him, almost a meditative retreat. When he wrote about it afterward, it was with nostalgia and gratitude. I willed his zen-like spirit to come to my aid but couldn't get past the blare of the sports radio program back at the sergeant's desk.

Thoreau ended up in a Concord jail because he chose not to pay his poll tax; he didn't want to support a government that still allowed slavery. I, on the other hand, had disregarded a sign saying NO DOGS ALLOWED. And it wasn't even my dog! How did I have the nerve to compare myself to such an American icon? Because I owned a small number of possessions and hung out in the woods? The essay he wrote about that fateful night, "Civil Disobedience," had influenced and empowered men from Gandhi to Dr. Martin Luther King Jr. Thoreau's piece had changed the world, while my incoherent notes wouldn't even make it to first draft.

Pacing the small cell, I asked myself what cause *was* important enough to go to prison for. I used to have principles I'd give my freedom to defend, but none of them came to mind now. I was a joke as a guru *and* a disciple.

I woke up early and wondered if Peter, Beth, or Janine had gotten my messages. The tiny cell made me miss the long strides I'd taken while surveying; the morning light begged to be painted, even on one of Gus's paint-by-numbers canvases.

Janine finally showed up, frantic with worry. "I tried calling you at home all morning. I've been through the woods for hours looking for Brady."

I told her Brady had spent the night in the town kennel. It bothered me that she seemed more worried about her dog than me. "I left you several messages. Where were you?"

"With Gus," she said. "You know that."

"And you just got my message *now*? Did you think I was going to dogsit for you all night while you hooked up with Gus?"

"Can we deal with this later, please? I need to see my dog." Janine waited as the officer unlocked my cell.[61] He waved me out and went back to his clipboard.

"Aren't you forgetting something?" I asked.

The officer flipped through his notes and apologized before handing me an envelope with my house key.[62]

"Hel-lo?" I said. "Can we have our dog?"

"The collie? What a shame. Such a beautiful animal." The officer shook his head.

"What do you mean 'what a shame'?" Janine's voice sounded shriller than a teakettle at full steam.

"He was acting strange on the way to the kennel, then bit the owner's son."

"Brady's never bitten anyone!"

---

[61] Because Janine was so worried about Brady and I was feeling like such a loser, I didn't run through the lines I'd been practicing all night. When Emerson went to the prison the next day to see Thoreau, he asked him, "Henry, what are you doing in there?" Thoreau supposedly answered, "Waldo, what are you doing out *there*?" Their Abbott and Costello routine didn't seem appropriate given Janine's state of mind.

[62] I told you I traveled light.

"Well, he did yesterday. A six-year-old boy who's potentially facing a painful series of rabies shots. We called the number on his collar all day, but no one answered. When we told the state coordinator at the Department of Public Health we had a possible rabies case involving a child, an AWOL owner, and an incarcerated dogsitter, he instructed us to euthanize the dog immediately."

Janine lunged toward the officer; I grabbed her clenched fists.

"Whoa, young lady," the officer said. "We waited as long as we could. I'm very sorry."

I felt terrible about Brady, but a minuscule slice of evil inside me smirked at Janine having to pay such a high price for her overnight with Gus. I felt terrible squared, though, as she began to sob through her explanation.

"I was at Mass General . . . getting stuck with needles . . . to see if I could donate an organ . . . to someone I don't even know. They made me shut off my cell. . . . My dog's never bitten anyone . . . in his life. I can't remember his last shot . . . but he's not rabid."

"We'll find out soon enough." The officer seemed sympathetic but ready to move on with his day.

I led Janine to the door and told the cop to let us know the results of the blood test.

"You can't test rabies from an animal's blood. The only reliable ID for rabies is brain tissue."

Janine started crying all over again. "Before you stick a needle into my dead dog's brain to test for a disease he doesn't have, can I at least see him to say goodbye?"

The man rubbed the back of his neck. "You can, but I'm not really sure you want to. You know, without his head."

"WHAT?" This time we both screamed.

The cop looked confused. "How else do you think the state lab gets brain tissue? We packed the head in dry ice this morning and sent it in."

Instead of lunging for the cop, this time Janine lunged for me. "You watch my dog for a few hours and he gets DECAPITATED?"

You know how sometimes your mind isn't in full synchronization with your mouth and you say something you immediately want to hit "rewind" on? Something like this: "I told you Brady shouldn't be at the pond. I told you hanging out with Gus was trouble. This is all *your* fault."

My words hit her like a left hook to the solar plexus.

"You obsess about Gus and me, you piss off a park ranger, my dog is decapitated on your watch—while I'm trying to donate my kidney to a stranger—and it's MY fault?" She grabbed the stapler from the officer's desk and threw it at me.

The cop must've thought she'd been through enough because he picked up the stapler from the floor without a word.

"Come on," I told Janine. "I'll drive you home."

Instead, she climbed into her car, locked the passenger door, and raced out of the parking lot without me.

Ever have one of those days—or weeks or months—where every person you know hates you? Maybe even people you don't know?

Janine hadn't spoken to me in the week since the incident. The fact that the state lab determined Brady didn't have rabies made her loss that much worse. The other students were almost as horrified. Katie was so disgusted with me, she forgot any petty disagreements she and Janine had and doted on her like a hospice nurse. When Mike made a bad joke about Brady following in his owner's footsteps by donating an organ of his own, his ostracism from the group was immediate.

Gus was the only one who seemed to take the episode in stride. He told us to move on and not incite the drama even further. He also insisted Janine withdraw herself from the donor process immediately. He spent a lot of time "comforting" her, but I didn't dare say a word. Playing Marie Antoinette's executioner with someone else's dog denies you the moral high ground.

Peter was angry too. He'd been in Portland pitching a gig for his events-planning company when I'd called him from jail. He made several phone calls to the Concord Police to try and wipe the charges from my permanent record, but because of a new online national criminal database, Princeton had already gotten wind of my arrest.

"If you blew your college career, there'll be hell to pay." Peter tried to keep the anger from his voice without success. "And Janine's dog—are you kidding? It'll be a miracle if she ever talks to you again."

Keep it coming. I deserve all the grief you dish out.

When Peter finally finished, I grabbed my jacket and went outside. I was surprised to find Beth sitting on the front steps.

"I could hear him from the driveway," Beth said. "Figured I'd wait for you out here." She leaned back to soak up the unseasonably warm November day.

"Why does all this stuff keep happening?" I asked. "Am I cursed?"

"Things happen to people every day—life, death, illness, good news, bad news. Stop thinking everything has to do with you." She handed me the stack of letters the mailman had given her.

I stared at the letter with the Princeton return address. "I guess those apologetic phone calls I made to their admissions director didn't do any good."

"Maybe it's just a bill," Beth said.

I appreciated her optimism, but it wasn't warranted. Princeton had rescinded their offer to have me attend in January.

Beth grabbed the letter from my hand. "You can fight it. Hire a lawyer."

"Peter's broke, and so am I."

"Doesn't running for president trump a twenty-four-hour arrest?"

But that accomplishment belonged to the old me, the me who had a firm grasp on his goal in life, who knew how to contribute. *This* Josh, this Larry, got innocent dogs decapitated, spent his stepfather's money on lecherous gurus, and couldn't find an epiphany to save his life. Princeton was right; I didn't belong there.

Beth pointed to another letter—this one from Massachusetts General Hospital. When she asked why they were writing to me, I shoved the letter into my pocket.

"I hope that's not what I think it is," she said.

"The forecast calls for snow, but it's too warm, don't you think?"

Beth didn't buy my change of subject. "Just because Janine's upset about Brady doesn't mean you have to take her place as an organ donor."

"Too late." I handed her the letter telling me I'd passed the initial screening tests.[63] "I have to stop focusing on my own problems and do something positive. It's not fair that some do-gooder dies because I killed Janine's dog. The least I can do is help someone else to live a better life."

Beth spent the next half hour trying to change my mind. I ignored her, then set up a time to meet the person who hopefully would have better luck than I with my DNA.

---

[63] They might not have been so willing to accept me if they'd seen me bored out of my mind in the examination room waiting for the doctor. Boredom beat out common sense, and I ended up sticking tongue depressors in my mouth for my own amusement. Luckily the doctor came in before I started on the Q-tips.

Although I didn't legally need his consent, in the end I was grateful to have Peter's blessing. He'd insisted on visiting his internist to see if his blood matched the chosen recipient to spare me from having to go through the ordeal of a transplant. He couldn't hide his disappointment when the test came back saying his blood wasn't a match. I hated playing the what-if-this-was-Mom card again, but I knew it would seal the deal. It did.

With Janine still not talking to me and Mike making Brady jokes behind her back, I finished the rest of the surveying alone. On my last tract of land, I spotted a squirrel rooting around the base of a giant pine. What I thought might be a cache of acorns turned out to be a cardboard cylinder filled with survey maps, many of them mine. Someone had made small x's on the maps' walking paths. Was Gus correcting our work? Why hadn't he told me I'd made mistakes, and why was he hiding the maps out here? I felt confused and unsure about turning them in; I was still on thin ice with the group. I decided to bury them back where I'd found them. When I finished, I could swear I saw the same tourist I'd seen with the videocamera a few weeks ago filming from the other side of the cove.

Mike yelled that Gus had arrived with the recipient, so we

all scrambled to the beach. The wind had picked up, and we wrapped our jackets and blankets even tighter around us. Gus started down the hill slowly, holding on to the woman who would receive my kidney. Because of the trees, I couldn't see her face but was surprised the charitable organization would offer an organ to someone old; I assumed they gave priority to patients with a longer life expectancy.

I hadn't seen Peter sitting by the boathouse; Katie waved him over, and he joined us on the beach. "This is a wonderful act of charity," Katie said. "You must be so proud of Larry."

"I am."

Mike passed around a bag of trail mix and bottles of water. I tried yet again to make eye contact with Janine, but when I did, she seemed catatonic. For the first time since Brady died, she made physical contact and grabbed my arm. "You need to see this." She pointed up the hill.

Peter wore the same ashen expression as Janine, so I jockeyed to get a better view. As Gus ushered the woman into the center of our circle, I dropped the bag of trail mix. Was this some kind of sick joke?

The woman continued to hold Gus's arm for support.

"I'd like to introduce a woman who leads a life of charity and love," Gus said. "Everyone, meet Tracy Hawthorne."

Neither Janine nor Peter uttered a sound. My mind raced with a hundred possible things to say, but no words came. After several awkward moments, I approached the person scheduled to receive my kidney.

"We've actually met," I told Gus. "But back then, she went by the name of betagold."

PART THREE

"Emancipate yourselves from mental slavery;
none but ourselves can free our minds."

Bob Marley
"Redemption Song"

"She tried to have you killed!" Beth shouted. "She set up Janine. You lost the election because of her!"

"Tell me something I don't know," I snapped. "I thought Janine was going to shove her into the pond."

"You are *not* going through with this operation," Peter said.

"Obviously," I said.

"Did Gus know about this?" Beth asked. "The guy knows everything else about your life. I bet he set this up on purpose."

I told her Gus denied knowing anything about my past history with betagold but I didn't believe him for a second.

"Is there any good news?" Beth asked. "Besides betagold being fatally ill?"

"I hate her," I said. "But I don't want her to die." I took my bowl of uneaten oatmeal to the sink. "I guess the good news is that Janine is talking to me again. Betagold has taken her mind off Brady, at least for a while."

"You should've seen betagold's face when she realized who the donor was," Peter told Beth. "You could see her hopes for a new kidney vanishing before her eyes. I almost felt bad for her."

"*That* would've been worth cutting drama class for," Beth said.

As much as I agreed with them, I felt that all the hate bouncing across the kitchen went directly against everything I believed in. I'd spent a lot of energy trying not to take betagold's obsession with my downfall personally, and all this talk stirred up those old negative feelings. As much as I didn't want to help betagold, I didn't want to hurt her, either. Life was too short. Maybe the weeks spent with Gus instead of on the couch were paying off.

Since Janine had actually spoken to me again, I decided to surprise her at Victopia. On the ride over, I replayed yesterday afternoon in my mind. After seeing me, betagold had talked about the grandchildren she'd like to spend more time with and the mistakes she'd made. But most of all, she talked about forgiveness. She held my eyes like a laser beam. By the end, she—and everyone else—was almost crying. Everyone except Janine, Peter, and me. Gus looked at me as if to say, "Well?" I walked past betagold up the hill to the parking lot without a word.

Katie seemed surprised when she answered the door at Victopia. It appeared as if Janine had just woken up; she held the door ajar with her foot.

"Aren't you going to invite me in?" I asked. You'd think volunteering to donate a major organ would get you off the commuting list.

"The house is a mess," Janine said. "Let me get dressed— we can go for a walk."

I peeked my head through the small space. "What's going on? Are you with Gus?"

"Will you stop? He's the only reason I'm keeping it together since Brady died."

Mike returned and asked me to help him stack wood; I felt as if he was babysitting me while Janine got ready. She emerged in a few minutes, and we hiked down the road to Walden.

"Can you imagine either of us giving a kidney to beta-gold?" Janine asked. "The organization double-checked her application—all that charitable work is true. I know it sounds sick, but I wouldn't be surprised if she planned this whole thing as some new way to mess around with your mind."

"Not to sound egotistical, but I was thinking the same thing. Of all the kidneys, in all the towns, in all the world, she signs up for mine."[64]

"Seventeen people die every day waiting for a kidney transplant. If a living donor doesn't volunteer, they have to wait for someone to die."

"Maybe betagold got tired of waiting for me to croak, and this is the closest she could get," I said.

When we came to Brady's favorite cove, Janine choked up.

"I'm so sorry," I said. "Maybe we can look on craigslist for a new puppy."

"I don't want a new puppy," she snapped. "I want Brady."[65]
She answered her cell on the first ring. "I was just thinking

---

[64] I was paraphrasing a line from *Casablanca*. Such a great film.

[65] I took her sharp tone as additional evidence she and I would not be getting back together anytime soon.

about you," she said. "Everywhere I turn, something reminds me of Brady. It's just so hard."

It didn't take me long to figure out she was talking to Gus. Brady's death had given him Janine's full emotional attention on a platter.[66] From my hiding place behind the nearest tree, I couldn't help but hear her make plans to meet Gus later.

"Didn't you just see him at the house?" I asked as we set out on our hike.

"He's been amazing. He was on the phone with my father last night being so supportive."

I felt a pang of envy for Janine, Mike, and Katie all playing utopian *Brady Bunch* in a giant Victorian with Gus. "Why was he talking to your dad?"[67]

"My parents were worried about me and wanted to make sure I was okay. Plus, Gus was talking to my father about some investments."

I stopped walking, as much to catch my breath as to find out more.

"My father's thinking of investing in some side projects with Gus. I don't know the details."

I told her about the survey plans I'd found hidden on the other side of the pond. "The last people who tried to develop land out here got shut down. I hope he's not taking your father for a ride."

"All I know is, I couldn't have dealt with losing Brady without him."

---

[66] No Saint John the Baptist jokes, please.

[67] Oh, yeah, your dad—the guy who wouldn't even let me in to use the bathroom when I finally reached Seattle last year looking for you.

Janine and I hiked the rest of the way in silence. I appreciated the fact that our relationship was wide enough to embrace
such mutual solitude.[68] The setting was idyllic and the brisk
pace invigorating, but I felt anxious. Was Janine getting in over
her head? Was Gus working a scam on her parents? As we
reached the crest and gazed down to the water below,
betagold seemed the least of my worries.

---

[68] Either that or she was still mad at me.

When I pulled my bike into the Walden parking lot the next day, the first person I saw was betagold. She was standing next to the bike rack; I had to avoid catching the tubes of her oxygen tank as I ran the cable and lock around the frame of my bike.

"My body is falling apart," she said. "But I have money and a specific blood type. Let me buy your kidney."

I told her selling an organ was against the law and I wasn't interested in joining the black market, thank you very much.

"What's in the past is done," she said.

"Because it's convenient for you? I don't think so." She had probably lost thirty pounds since I first met her; she looked gaunt and pale. I wished her good luck in finding another donor.

She put her hands on her knees and breathed deeply. Even though she'd ruined my life several times, I couldn't leave her in such pain. When I asked if she wanted me to call 911, she told me she had these spells several times a day.

"Look, I admit what I did was wrong," betagold said. "I apologize. Can't we leave it at that?"

"No, we can't. Now if you're feeling better, I'll be on my way."

When she grabbed me by the arm, her grip was weak. "How about if I offer you something better than money?"

"I doubt you have anything I need." I said goodbye and headed toward the pond.

After a moment, I turned around. She was dragging the oxygen tank behind her, trying to catch up. I waited by the cabin replica until she did.

"You know that hole in the woods you're so fond of?" she asked. "How about if I told you I know people on the zoning board who can preserve that land."

"Are you trying to bribe me into giving you my kidney?"

"Obviously."

"And how do you know about that hole?"

She told me she'd read my books.[69] "Don't think of it as a bribe. Think of it as an exchange." She dragged the oxygen tank up the step and sat on the replica of Thoreau's cot. When a group of tourists came by, betagold and I leaned back against the inside wall so as not to ruin their shot.[70]

"After taking care of my grandchildren, I'll leave the bulk of my estate to the charitable organization of your choice," betagold continued. "An anticonsumerism group, a foundation for people working in sweatshops, a nature conservancy." She took a deep breath from her oxygen mask. "You can come with me to the attorney's. She can adapt my will according to your requests." She looked me straight in the eye; as sick as she was, her blue eyes remained clear. "My estate is worth three

---

[69] She also said she didn't think she'd been accurately portrayed. I told her if she wanted to come off more likable, she should write her own books.

[70] I then volunteered to take a photo of two teachers from Oakland standing in front of the bronze statue of Thoreau with their stuffed animals. They said it was for a class project, but I didn't believe them.

million dollars now. That kind of money can sow a lot of good in the world."

"As much as I'd love to contribute to the betterment of the planet, my internal organs are not for sale." I watched her fight for each breath. She was just someone's grandmother, after all. "No offense, but I can't imagine part of me being part of you, no matter how much you pledge to charity."

"How about your criminal record? Or getting you reinstated at Princeton?"

"How do you know about that?"

"I know lots of things. You should know that my brother-in-law has been on the board there for years. Your academic future can be back on track with a phone call."

I lifted up my shirt and rubbed my back. Would I miss a kidney? Would it be worth giving up one of them to keep my favorite woods undeveloped, wipe my record clean, and get back into Princeton? Not to mention a substantial donation to a worthy charity. I leaned back in the tiny cabin and weighed the options. But even after several minutes of listening to betagold gasp for breath, I had to tell her no.

She took the news surprisingly well. "I know you hate me, but are you sure? Thoreau himself once wrote 'It is never too late to give up your prejudices.'"

"Thanks, but no thanks," I said.

She shook my hand and wished me well. When we got back to the parking lot, she reached into her fanny pack.[71] "You

---

[71] While I was traveling cross-country, I met a girl named Fanny Pack, I swear to God. Great body, bad name.

might want to see these." She handed me several photographs. Janine and Gus by the fire. Janine leaning her head on Gus's shoulder. Janine and Gus kissing.

I returned them to her. "You could've doctored these in Photoshop."

She went into her pack again and took out a digital camera. She scrolled through the stored images, identical to the photographs. "He's toying with her, taking advantage of his position as a teacher. Trying to rip her off."

The disturbing images confirmed my worst fear. The only good news was that as much as the thought of Janine and Gus infuriated me, it also meant I wasn't paranoid.

She held up the most incriminating picture.[72] "I can get him to stop seeing her tomorrow. All you have to do is agree to the operation."

"She's not my girlfriend anymore," I said. "She can do whatever she wants."

"Yes, but she's your *friend.* You love her. I guarantee you, he will mop the floor with her emotions. To say nothing of her parents' bank account. He is one tough Saudi Arabian."

I gave up trying to figure out Gus's ethnicity and instead asked betagold how she planned to get Janine away from him.

"He has his price, believe me."

I thought about everything Janine and I had been through. Was she really in trouble? Did I owe her this after accusing her of spying during the campaign? After killing her dog? Or was betagold up to something even more sinister this time around?

---

[72] I'm not going to tell you what it was, so don't ask.

When I looked at her now, though, she only seemed sick and old.

"Saving the land, wiping my record clean, Princeton, adjusting your will, and getting Gus to stop seeing Janine in exchange for my kidney? Is that it?"

"And I pick up all medical costs. That's what I'm offering."

I told her first I had to speak to Janine.

"But you'll consider it?" betagold asked.

"I will."

She seemed so relieved, I thought she might collapse. As I helped her into her van, I wondered if I'd just made a deal with the devil.

Cabin site of Henry David Thoreau at Walden Pond

I found Janine down by the beach. The hood of her sweatshirt was pulled tight around her face, and she carried a small metal container. When I asked what she was doing, she opened the box. Inside were chunks of ashes.

"Is that Brady?" I asked.

"Everything but his head.[73] At least he can be here legally now."

"He loved the pond. I can't think of a better resting place." I watched her sprinkle the ashes onto the cold, green water. The pond would be iced over in another few months. I imagined fishermen walking over Brady's frozen remains as they cut holes in his final resting place, the cycle of life and death.

The wind picked up, blowing bits of Brady on our clothes. I hurriedly brushed them off before Janine started crying again.

"Look what Gus made for me." She carefully removed a paint-by-numbers canvas of a collie from her pack. The acrylic looked grittier than our other paintings. "Gus mixed some of

---

[73] Ouch.

Brady's ashes into the paint so I could have a little bit of him with me forever."

"How thoughtful," I lied. The guy was a freak.

We stood for several minutes watching the gray debris float across the pond. I wondered if the koi would find their way to Brady's ashes. I waited several minutes before bringing up Gus again.

"You're spending a lot of time with him one-on-one," I said. "I worry about his motives."

"You should spend more time on your studies and less time worried about me."

I took a deep breath and told her about the photographs. When Janine turned to face me, she was furious. "Where did you see pictures of Gus and me?"

"Don't worry about where I saw them. Have you been with him or not?"

"Was it Katie? She's been pissed off about us from day one."

"Then it's true? There is a 'you and Gus'?"

She accused me of trying to trip her up linguistically, then asked me again where I'd seen the pictures.

"Betagold," I answered.

The veins on the sides of her head looked ready to explode. "How short is your memory? Did you forget she framed me once before? She's obviously doing it again!"

"The photographs were on her camera. I saw them." I reached for her hands, but she pushed me away. "I'm trying to *help* you."

"This is what Gus said you'd do if you found out about us," Janine said. "Try to make it seem like a bad thing."

"It *is* a bad thing! He's old, he's gross, he's supposed to be your teacher!"

"I'm eighteen," she said. "I can take care of myself."

"Obviously not. The thought of you kissing Mr. Garlic Guru makes me sick."[74]

When I reached for her once more, she pushed me so hard I fell backward with her on top of me.

"I hate you," she said. "You believe betagold instead of me—again."

I tried to hold her, but she broke free and ran up the trail.

"I just want to help you get away from him," I yelled.

"The only person I want to get away from is you."

I could've chased her. I didn't. Maybe we weren't a couple anymore, but a spare kidney seemed a small price to pay for saving one of the most important people in my life from imminent pain. I took no pleasure in donating my kidney to betagold, but it would certainly make me happy to get Janine away from Gus.

I rode home and called Mass General Hospital.

---

[74] P.S.—What about kissing *me*?

102

When Peter heard I was bartering my future with my old neme-sis, he was apoplectic with anger.[75] Katie was pretty much the only one who approved of my decision to help betagold. I wasn't so sure but needed all the encouragement I could get.

The private investigator called as soon as I walked in the door from the day's lesson with Gus. "Boy, you sure know how to pick 'em," she said.

"What do you mean?"

"Gus Muldarian—eighteen months for fraud, an acquittal for black-market smuggling in Syria, another fifteen months for forging checks."

I imagined Peter's money in neat stacks on a casino table while the ball bounced inside a roulette wheel from one wrong number to the next.

"There's an open warrant out on him in Ohio," the detective said. "He was arrested for drunk and disorderly conduct but jumped bail. I'm still trying to get to the bottom of all the aliases."

"Anything to do with cults?"

---

[75] We won't even talk about Beth.

"No, but he used to work in a halfway house in Columbus for teen runaways," the woman answered. "Until he started harassing the underage women."

The thought made me nauseous until I realized I'd made the right decision about getting Janine away from Gus.

"Did you find anything *good* on him? Took care of a sick relative? Volunteered at an AIDS clinic?" I could hear the detective shuffling through stacks of papers. "Did I get you at a bad time?"

"You know how it is when you get back from vacation. Ah, here we go. He drank himself across the Midwest before passing out somewhere near Cleveland. People actually thought he was dead. He used the opportunity to create a new identity, of course."[76]

"Cleveland? That's strange. That's where my father died."

"Maybe they were drinking buddies. This guy's got an alias for every day of the week. Gus Muldarian, John Shalhoub, Thomas Swensen."

"Swensen? That's *my* name."

"Point is, you should be careful with this guy."

I could barely hear her with the phone dangling from my hand. What if Gus had used Thomas Swensen, my real father's name, as an alias the way I'd used Gil Jackson when I chose a new identity? Or was Gus actually my . . . I couldn't let the word form inside me. But the coincidences were striking: both from Cleveland, both drinkers, both the same age, both with the name Swensen. When I'd faked my own death, I

---

[76] Sound familiar?

thought the idea was mine, but maybe I had just unwittingly followed in my father's footsteps: a pseudocidal biological imperative. Hiding from who we really are—like father, like son. I ran to the bathroom, thinking I might vomit. If Gus was my biological father, was he aware I was his son? Was that why he had my name in his pocket that first day? Was he hitting on my ex-girlfriend while knowing he's my father? My mother had never given me details of my father's life; maybe she was trying to protect me from a man with a dangerous past. The whole thing creeped me out on so many levels. I wanted to find another identity and become someone else immediately.

I pulled down the rickety stairs to the attic and made my way through the boxes of Peter's records and books until I found my mother's old brown leather photo albums. Faded color photographs of Mom in college dressed up as the Tin Man from *The Wizard of Oz*. A photo of her pulling me in my little wagon to the playground at the top of the street.[77] A man with a beard and round glasses making a peace sign into the camera. The gesture didn't belong to either of us, of course, but the fact that my biological father and I shared the same greeting suddenly felt more ancestral than accidental. His other hand held a six-pack of beer. It was impossible to tell if this young man had morphed into Gus through the years.

From the bottom of the stairs, Peter wondered if I was okay. I asked him what my mom had told him about my biological father.

---

[77] She thought the typical red wagon was too boring and had painted mine lime green. I remember feeling like I was riding a glowworm all the way to the playground.

He shrugged. "From what she said, he was some big radical who had a few screws loose. Nice guy but always trying to fight the system. Why do you want to know?"

I ignored the question and asked him what year my father had died.

Peter climbed the stairs and sat beside me on the wide-planked floor. "Right before you were born. I think he had alcohol poisoning and drowned."

I banged my head against the rafter several times. "My mother always spared me the gruesome details, but did they ever find his body?"

"Your mother never held any false hopes he was alive. You shouldn't either."

I went back and forth but decided not to tell Peter about my conversation with the detective. He lifted one of the photos from the box—my mother standing in the driveway after one of her many chemo appointments. With her black-and-white sweater, pale skin, and thin frame, she looked like an escaped inmate from the local prison. Peter gazed at the photograph and smiled. "I miss her every day."

Join the club. I stared at the photo, wishing she could advise me on what to do with my new "teacher." I rarely thought about my biological father, but for the rest of the night, I could think of nothing else. And if it did turn out to be Gus, what kind of game was he playing?

I took the bus to Providence to talk to Beth. Her dorm room was filled with stacks of open books, and her bulletin board was so full of notes and photos not a glimpse of cork could be found. She hurried to clear a space for me on her bed. When I told her about my conversation with the detective the day before, she held up her hand to stop me.

"I never would've given you the detective's name if I'd known she was going to give you false hope about your father. What did Peter say?"

"I didn't tell him about Gus."

"Well, don't," Beth said. "I guarantee it's a giant mistake. The part about being your father, I mean."

"Don't you think I should ask Gus if he is my biological father?"

"*No!* This is so you, picking at a scab until it bleeds.[78] Just leave it alone."

"I never leave things alone—you know that."

When Beth sat next to me on the bed, her eyes were filled with concern. "You're so much better than you were a few

---

[78] A very bad habit of mine.

months ago. You're almost back to your old self. I don't want to see you backslide again because of some . . . mistake."

I told her she was the one who told me to call the detective in the first place.

"Just promise you won't overfocus on it, okay? You've got enough going on right now." I could almost see the gears of her brain clicking as she spoke. "Maybe you'll fail the psych evaluation at Mass General and you won't have to donate your kidney, after all."

I ignored her. "Walk me to the bus—I've got to get back."

Even when we fight, Beth and I never stay mad at each other for long.[79] She wrapped her scarf around her neck three times and walked me to the bus station.

Betagold kept her word. When I got home, Princeton admissions had called to reinstate me. Then after a few closed-door meetings between the developer and zoning board, the bulldozer was removed from my favorite woods. Betagold's attorney sent me a copy of the revised will, leaving two million dollars to several grassroots political organizations. The only thing left was getting Janine away from Gus. I don't know what betagold offered our teacher, but he set Janine adrift the next day.

"What did I do wrong?" Janine asked me. "Things with Gus were going so well." She wiped her eyes with the back of her hand. "You did this, didn't you?"

I didn't answer, just sat next to her on the wall and listened to her cry. I decided not to tell her about Gus's record, guessing it would only make things worse.

---

[79] Okay, maybe a few times.

"I suppose we didn't have much of a chance anyway," she finally said. "Gus is so obsessed with his work, he barely had any time for me. He set up a large tent way back in the woods, a makeshift office full of diagrams and notebooks. I wonder if it has anything to do with those survey maps you found."

I asked her if she'd examined any of the diagrams. She said every time she tried, one of the other students came in. "Will you be honest with me?" she asked.

"Absolutely."

"Promise me Gus breaking up with me had nothing to do with betagold."

I kept my mouth shut.

"You're not giving her your kidney, are you?"

More silence.

She jumped up. "She doesn't deserve it!"

"A deal is a deal. Even with betagold."

"She doesn't have that many years left," Janine said. "If you're going to mutilate yourself, at least give a new life to someone worthy."

"She might have twenty years. That's a lot of time to watch your grandchildren grow up."

The same tourist from several weeks ago was shooting video footage again.

"Do you mind?" I asked. "This is a private conversation."

"Oops, sorry." The man scurried down the hill toward the beach.

"Don't you think that guy's following us?" I asked.

"There are people with cameras here all the time. What makes you think it's the same guy?"

"Same bushy mustache, same Yankees hat—doesn't he look familiar?"

Janine tossed back her hair. "Come on, let's grab some lunch."

"Maybe he's doing an exposé on Gus," I said. "Maybe Gus is about to get busted."

"Maybe you should donate your imagination to science instead of your kidney—you've got enough to spare."

I watched the man hurry down the path and wondered what he'd found here that was worth documenting.

I thought the hospital would've needed a battery of procedures—CT scan, chest X-ray, tissue typing—but the surgeon said my blood showed a perfect match, and they'd perform any last-minute tests before the surgery. I figured betagold had bought her way into this streamlined program. The instructions from Mass General said not to eat after midnight, so I ate a huge bowl of pasta for dinner that night. The next morning, the only liquid allowed was a sip of water to wash down the sedatives.

"I don't see why I need these now," I told Peter. "I'll be getting general anesthesia at the hospital."

"They probably want to keep you relaxed. Did they give you any extra?" Peter held out his hand, but I'd already swallowed the pills. "I can't say I agree with you on this one, but I know your mother would be proud. Plus, the money from betagold's estate will do a lot of good in the world."

Beth took the passenger seat, and I crawled in back. As we drove to Mass General, it didn't take long for the drugs to kick in. But even facing major surgery, I couldn't help think about the possibility that Gus might be my biological father. After spending the years following my mother's death obsessing about having no blood relatives, suddenly here was a real possibility—and I wasn't sure I liked it. What if my father was a criminal? What if those same destructive genes were inside me? The private investigator had called back to say the assistant she'd used during her vacation had provided unreliable information about Gus.

"He never used the name Swensen," she said. "I'm sure he's not your father."

But that didn't stop me from dwelling on the possibility anyway.

"Whoa, buddy. Let me give you a hand." Peter grabbed me as I stumbled into pre-op.

A woman and two men in scrubs led me to a gurney. I stayed focused by watching the bright lights bounce off the stainless steel. Gus suddenly appeared in my field of vision, looking at me with an expression of compassion. "You're doing something wonderful here. Taking your studies to another level."

Peter moved his body between Gus and me. "We're all set here, Gus. We'll give you a call after the surgery."

Gus nodded agreeably, but when Peter went to talk to the surgeon, I grabbed him by the arm. I wanted to ask about Cleveland and the name Swensen. Instead I asked if I could have one of his bracelets for good luck. Gus removed one of the elastics from his wrist and handed it to me. He saw Peter watching us and exited the room. I handed the elastic to Beth.

"Have them run a paternity test on this. Gus's hair is all over it."

"You're on drugs—literally. The private investigator said it was a screwup. Let it go!" Still, she took the elastic.

"If they don't do testing here, find a place on the Internet. Some of them get you results in just a few days." I yanked out one of my own hairs and gave it to her. I also made her promise not to tell Peter.

"Betagold's in the next room yelling, being a total bitch." Beth rubbed her hand across my arm and told me I could still back out.

But I was committed to going through with the deal. By the time the tech came to wheel me into the operating room, Beth was crying. "This reminds me of when you got hit by the car. I'll be here waiting this time too."

At that moment, I felt nothing but love for Beth, but it might've been the drugs. I squinted into the lights behind the surgeon. Even with his surgical mask and cap, his eyes were smiling. "Everything's going to be okay. You're doing fine."

As I went under, I had a vision of my mother. She was wearing a gladiator outfit—breastplate, sword, shield, the whole warrior thing. I knew nothing bad would happen with her on guard. I thought I heard a dog barking too—maybe Brady was helping Mom patrol the universe. I drifted off to sleep.

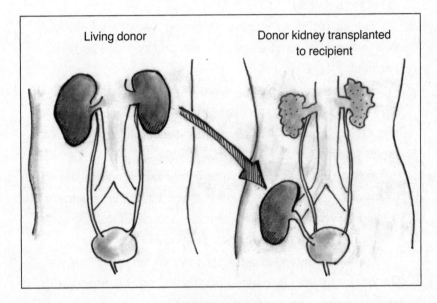

Living donor

Donor kidney transplanted
to recipient

Kidney transplant

When I woke up, the first person I saw was Peter. He was leaning over the hospital bed looking as concerned as I've ever seen him.

"You kept saying 'Dad, Dad.' I was beginning to worry."

I made the groggy decision not to tell Peter about Gus.

"The surgeon said everything went well. No complications."

"Where am I?"

"You're in your room—you slept through most of post-op. The surgeon says you'll be here only two to three days, if you can believe it."

The IV and adjustable bed made an interesting contrast with the flowered drapes.

"No complaining about the decor," Beth said. "At least betagold sprang for a single room." She held a cup of ice water and straw to my lips.

"She's still in surgery," Peter said. "I guess it's a lot more complicated on her end."

When I reached toward the large gauze that covered my back, Peter grabbed my hand. "The bandages have to stay on for two weeks." He motioned with his head toward the hall.

"Gus has been camped out in the waiting room since they wheeled you in. The guy may be a kook, but I think he really cares about you."

I was overcome by thirst and asked for more water. A young nurse with an Irish accent left a pitcher on the table next to me. Besides being tired, I felt like my old self. Maybe life with only one kidney would be no big deal.

Janine arrived that afternoon.[80] She handed me several new paint kits, each tackier than the next—a jolly Santa, a cat stuck in a tree,[81] parrots in a rain forest. The rhythm of the painting process would hopefully keep my mind occupied during this time of rest. For someone who had lived in front of the television two months ago, I barely turned it on.

A different surgeon came by to check my incision and told me the sutures were internal and would dissolve within a week. I was itching to cruise the halls,[82] but each nurse insisted I remain in my room.

"Isn't walking good for your circulation?" I asked.

"It is," the male nurse with the multiearring lobes said. "From here to the bathroom, that's all."

When Gus came by to visit the next day, I welcomed the diversion. Even though the temperature outside was in the forties, Gus's Hawaiian shirt was unbuttoned; he wore sandals with no socks and tiny oval sunglasses. He offered me a Slim

---

[80] I wondered if it would be weird for her to run into Beth, but they chatted together like old friends.

[81] Have you ever seen a real cat stuck in a tree? I never have. Gotta be a myth.

[82] Contrary to what my feisty Haitian nurse may say, I was *not* trying to set up a slalom IV race.

Jim, but I declined. Gus placed a chess piece in my hand—a queen, even more delicately carved than the rook. "I should've carved a whole set by now, but I've been crazy busy," he said. "Things should taper off soon."

He poked through the get-well cards Beth had propped on the windowsill. "Tracy's doing great too," he said. "Seems like you two were made for each other."

I tried not to cringe.

He tore off another chunk of meat stick, then flipped through the paintings I'd made in yesterday's burst of activity. "You've really embraced this spiritual practice. Good for you." He used the Slim Jim as a pointer, highlighting different areas of the canvases. "Right here, for example. What did painting this sail teach you?"

The crisp off-white and pale yellow of the sails brought me back immediately to my state of mind as I painted them. My initial thought was to censor my response to Gus, but that hardly seemed the best strategy in dealing with one's teacher. "I was thinking about Janine. Worried she was getting too close to you, using you as a crutch." I forced myself to keep going. "Worried you were taking advantage of her."

"Good! You really followed your mind." He didn't seem put off in the least that I'd just accused him of manipulating Janine. He shoved the stubby snack at the next painting. "And this one?"

Gus pointed to a cowboy sitting on a fence with a guitar. Getting the paisley of the guy's shirt just right had taken me the entire morning. I weighed my words carefully.

"When I painted that cowboy, I was thinking about my biological father. How I wished I'd known him."

Gus motioned toward a photograph of Peter and me on the nightstand that Beth had brought from home the day before. "Trouble in Dad-town?"

"It has nothing to do with Peter," I answered. "Just about me knowing my place in the world."

He sat on the edge of the hospital bed. "You need to know where your biological father is before you know your place in the world? Doesn't that have more to do with you than with him?"

As I got up the nerve to ask the most important question of my life, the nurse came in to take my blood pressure. I waited to see if Gus flirted with the young woman, but he didn't. On her way out, she handed me a stack of mail and magazines Peter had dropped off while I was asleep. I grabbed the overnight letter with the DNA testing logo and ripped it open. Gus walked around the bed and read over my shoulder.

"Seems the sample you sent wasn't good enough." He pulled back his hair into a ponytail. "Hair samples, for example. You've got to yank it out by the root. It's the follicle that has all the DNA information, not the strand. Most people don't realize that."

I stared at the words INCONCLUSIVE RESULTS.[83] I'd invested so many hours in this test being definitive, yet I never considered I could end up right back where I'd started. I'd gone through dozens of scenarios in my head and felt that either way I could deal with the results. What I couldn't deal with was *not* knowing.

---

[83] Perfect title for my autobiography.

I decided to confront Gus directly. "I sent them *your* hair samples. I thought you might be my father."

He nodded gently and told me that over the years, many of his disciples felt that way.

"This isn't a case of admiring a teacher and wishing he were your parent," I said. "Is it an accident you came into my life, that you had my name in your pocket as if you were looking for me?"

He picked up the stack of paintings. "There are no accidents. You know that."

"Well? Are you my father or not?"

"We're all on this earth to take care of each other."

"Can the mumbo jumbo, Gus. Yes or no, it's a simple question."

He balanced the paintings on his hip. "Nothing simple about it at all. Nonattachment, remember, son?"

The encounter left me shaken; my scar throbbed. But the pain from the incision couldn't compare to the word Gus had used now pulsating inside my head: *son.*

I was excited to finally be home. Even though my hospital stay was less than three days, I'd missed the outdoors immensely. I spent my first afternoon in the backyard just taking in the brisk November air. With each cleansing exhalation, I tried to remove anxious thoughts—the inconclusive DNA test and Gus's outstanding Ohio warrant.

Janine walked across the side yard and sat next to me on the picnic table. Her down jacket made her seem as if she'd been swallowed by a gray quilted balloon. It was still jarring to see her without Brady by her side.

"Something's up with Gus," she said. "UPS trucks have been coming and going from the house all week. He set up a bank of laptops in the dining room, and all the students—except you and me, who are obviously being kept out of the loop—are scurrying around like Santa's elves on Christmas Eve. I have no idea what's going on."

"Maybe it has something to do with this." Beth cut through the house and joined us in the yard, wielding her laptop and a pissed-off expression. "I was looking online to find you a present to celebrate your recovery."

"You were?"

"Don't get too excited—this is more important." Beth tilted the screen toward us. "I wanted to find you some new paint-by-numbers kits, since you're obsessed with the stupid things, but look what I found instead." She brought up a Web site selling artwork from Sudanese refugees.

"What's the big deal?" I asked.

"This." Beth scrolled through the paintings for sale—a napping Santa, a kitten in a tree, a parrot in the jungle, a cowboy playing guitar.

"There's Katie's painting of the autumn landscape and Mike's sunset." Janine shrieked when she saw the ballet dancers she'd slaved over the week before.

"Your guru isn't burning your paintings," Beth said. "He's pretending they were done by orphans and telling people the money goes to charity. He's probably pocketing the profit too."

"This explains the boxes, the computers, the UPS trucks." A wave of anger took over Janine's face. "He's supposed to be our teacher!"

Beth shot me a "don't even think about saying he might be your father" look, so instead I stared at the image of the cowboy and his meticulously rendered shirt.[84] Not only was Gus lying about who'd painted it, he was charging four hundred and fifty dollars for "authentic ethnic art"! Potential buyers had

---

[84] Even with a screen resolution of 640 × 480, the thing looked *great*.

no way of knowing the painting had been done not by a Sudanese orphan but by a soon-to-be Ivy League teen from Massachusetts.

"And this page is linked to another shopping site. Look!" Janine cried. "My Gore-Tex jacket, Katie's skateboard, Mike's laptop."

"I hate to say I told you so," Beth said, "but he's a con artist. Preaching no possessions and nonattachment, then selling your stuff online and keeping the money. Give me a break."

"Devil's advocate," I said. "Nothing on either of these sites mentions Gus's name or address. It seems like he's behind it, but we can't prove it." Still, Janine and I agreed to confront him. I hoped for a more definitive answer than he'd given me on the paternity issue.

When we reached Walden, betagold almost knocked me over with her enthusiasm.

"I'm alive because of you," she said. "The antirejection drugs haven't made me sick, and I'm feeling more like myself every day.[85] Your youthful energy is giving me strength. I thank my stars Gus brought us together. I've joined your group now too."[86]

"I'm glad you're feeling better," I said.

"Better? Look at this." She vaulted over a small stump

---

[85] I'm not sure that's a good thing.
[86] Ditto the last footnote.

twenty yards away. I began to wonder if my kidney had super powers, and if so, why they'd never manifested in me.[87]

"Gotta go," betagold said. "Gus gave me an assignment, and I don't want to let him down." When she pulled open the side of her vehicle, Janine and I both let out a gasp.

The entire floor of the van was stacked with boxes, packing tape, and our paint-by-numbers canvases.

---

[87]Maybe it was because betagold had three kidneys now; in most transplant cases, they attach the healthy, new kidney without bothering to remove the old one unless it's decayed. Ah, the wonders of technology.

Paint-by-numbers horse

Thanksgiving has never been one of my favorite holidays,[88] but it's the time of year Peter truly shines. He spends days working on his "turducken"—a chicken stuffed inside a duck stuffed inside a turkey. We've had many discussions over the years about such a gluttonous meat-fest, but I finally realized this extravagant, overblown fowl lies at the heart of Peter enjoying Thanksgiving. As he spent hours deboning and restuffing all three birds, I hid in the living room to escape the carcasses.

Katie had called to wish me a happy holiday and to tell me that betagold was spending the day with her grandchildren, thanks to me. I still didn't like betagold—especially after seeing the vanload of fraudulent art.

Janine and I had spent the past two days trying to track down Gus after seeing those canvases; whether it was the holiday or another excuse, he was nowhere to be found. Beth insisted he'd flown the coop, but I thought, naively or not, that he wouldn't leave without saying goodbye. I'd already decided to devote the rest of the long weekend to looking for him.

---

[88]Between missing my mother and not eating meat, it's always hard for me to get up the requisite appetite and cheer.

Peter stuck his head into the room waving the cleaver. "You sure you don't want to see this? It's a work of art, if I do say so myself."

For the hundredth time, I politely declined.

"No offense, but that tofurkey you're planning on eating doesn't hold a candle to this thing." He asked if I'd help him crisp the skin the way I always did. It took the two of us to carry the roasting pan into the backyard. We placed the turducken skin side down on the grate of the gas grill.

"The broiler is fine for most birds but not for this bad boy," he said.

I ran inside for my homemade gizmo—a combination of the old ignition from Peter's Jeep, a television remote, and a few odds and ends from Radio Shack. We both took cover behind the picnic table. I aimed the device at the gas grill and hit "enter." The flames rose more than three feet in the air.

"Even higher than last year," Peter cried.

I lowered the "volume" of the flame, then, when Peter gave the sign several minutes later, remotely shut off the grill. We approached the bird carefully.

"I could never get a fire that hot without singeing myself into the next county," Peter said. He used a long fork to turn the bird over. The skin had formed a mahogany crust. Peter wouldn't let us bring it inside until I'd taken a photograph of him with his culinary creation.

As we ate together in the dining room,[89] I wondered if a two-person Thanksgiving was intimate or pathetic. But Peter

_____

[89] I had to prop up an atlas between us to spare myself the sight of the carved bird.

was so animated and funny that I felt bad for even thinking such a thing. I also felt sorry I'd invested so much time trying to find out if Gus was my biological father. The one sitting right here in front of me didn't need much improvement at all.

When we cleaned up afterward, I couldn't help but notice the animal parts strewn across the counter. The tableau seemed almost violent, not the homey Thanksgiving that Norman Rockwell had envisioned. In his famous work, *Freedom from Want,* a loving grandmother places a large turkey in front of happy family and friends.[90] The response to Rockwell's Freedom series was so great the paintings ended up on national tour, raising morale and $130 million in war bonds.

But just as the Rockwell painting didn't show the family dysfunction behind the holiday, the paintings we did for Gus had untold stories too. Rockwell had raised money for the troops in World War II. What cause was Gus raising money for?

---

[90]My memory from art class is spotty, but I don't believe it was a turducken.

In between looking for Gus at Victopia and Walden on Saturday, I killed some time at the Concord Free Library. Down in the Special Collections room, I stood in awe of Thoreau's own compass. With its heavy wooden tripod and large brass face, it was no wonder it took two people to carry. The compass was understandably encased in Plexiglas, but I longed to touch it. Instead, I thumbed through Thoreau's copy of Charles Davies's *Elements of Surveying and Navigation.* Although the book had been written more than a hundred sixty years ago, the logarithms and formulas popped right off the page.[91] Holding the same volume Thoreau had used to check his calculations humbled me to the core. The librarian even showed me Thoreau's original survey maps. Similar to the copies Gus had printed online, these somehow seemed simpler, more workmanlike. Getting to hold these sacred manuscripts in my hands offset the fact that I still hadn't located Gus.

---

[91] I hate to use the word *giddy* but can't think of a better way to express my excitement at such rigorous mathematics.

On my way out of the library, I grabbed flyers for a local yoga class, a writing workshop,[92] and a seminar on nonviolence.

I finally found Gus sitting atop the pile of devotional stones at Thoreau's house site.[93] He sat in full lotus position; even with his eyes closed, he knew I was the one standing before him.

"You're here about the paintings, aren't you? Just because I burned the first one doesn't mean I burned the rest."

"You're lying about who painted them and profiting from the proceeds," I said. "Hardly a lesson in impermanence."

"You painted them, and they're gone," he said. "Seems pretty impermanent to me."

I asked how much money he'd made selling our paintings and possessions, then nearly fell over when he told me twelve thousand dollars.

"If you add in your two-thousand-dollar tuition plus Ms. Hawthorne's three thousand for me to stay away from Janine, that's a lot of cash," he said.

I felt like playing King of the Hill[94] and knocking him off his exalted position on the cairn. Instead, I asked him what he planned on doing with the money.

"Drinking heavily." He finally opened his eyes. "Didn't you say that was one of the things your father and I had in common?"

I was in no mood for jokes and asked him again what he was planning. He told me he was financing a pet project—nothing I needed to worry about. From atop his perch, Gus surveyed the

---

[92] Maybe some Concord teacher had tips for getting an ex-writer like me from note-taking to final draft stage again.

[93] It was hard to be there without thinking of Brady.

[94] For the first time in my life.

woods and pond below. "I'm expanding my views on Thoreau. Interpreting the texts a bit differently."

"What are you talking about?"

"Take 'A Plea for Captain John Brown.' In that famous speech, Thoreau said, 'I do not wish to kill nor to be killed, but I can foresee circumstances in which both these things would be by me unavoidable.'"

"He was saying maybe he could understand using violence to abolish slavery," I said. "He never *acted* on it."

"Maybe that was his weakness," Gus suggested. "Take you, for example—you acted on your belief that people should help others. You didn't just talk or write about it, you *did* something about it. At the end of his life, even Thoreau realized sometimes you might have to use violence to make a point."

When Gus put his hand on my shoulder, all the thoughts that he could be my biological father flooded in. As if he could read my mind, he told me not to ask him about it again. Then he picked up the shovel leaning against the tree and headed down the path. "You need to stop worrying so much," he called over his shoulder. "Life's just a game, remember?"

He walked down the hill. Then I watched him dig a hole on the narrow path while betagold measured the depth with a stick. She'd certainly made a nice recovery from the transplant. Since the operation, I found myself getting tired more often and having to stop and catch my breath. After all I'd gone through for her, maybe she could tell me what Gus was up to.

Gus's truck was parked in the back row of the parking lot. Knowing Gus, I figured it would be unlocked; it was. Coffee cups, candy wrappers, and envelopes tumbled to the ground when I opened the door. The mail was addressed to Doug Cri-mini. How many aliases did Gus have? A twin mattress covered with books and clothes was sandwiched in the corner of the van. A miner's helmet, caked with dirt, sat on the front seat. I hit the power switch and light filled the back of the truck. Tucked behind the front seat was a large box. It seemed to be the only thing in the truck with any sense of order. The box was filled with three large canisters that looked similar to metal canteens. I picked one up and looked for markings but couldn't find any. I put the cylinders back and closed up the truck.

As I unlocked my bike, the answer hit me like a thunderbolt from Zeus himself. Surveying the land, marking *x*'s on the maps, the shovels, the sudden talk of violence—they were all linked to those canisters.

I ran to the nearest phone to call Peter. If I was right, Gus's plans were a thousand times worse than anything I'd imagined.

"Land mines!" Peter said. "That's impossible!"

I brought up several images online—many of them looked like the devices I'd seen in Gus's truck. "That's why Gus had us survey the entire area. I bet he plans on burying the mines where he marked the *x*'s."

"There's absolutely no reason to put land mines at Walden Pond!"

"There's no reason to put land mines anywhere!" The why was the one part of Gus's plan I couldn't explain. But the more research I did, the more afraid I became.[95]

"Listen to this," I said. "Five million new land mines continue to be bought and buried every year, some for as little as three dollars apiece. Seems like Gus has a lot of company."

Peter shook his head. "I had no idea!"

There was no way to tell if Gus had already laid any mines or if the cache in his truck was the first. But even if I stole the modified survey maps to see where Gus planned to bury

---

[95] Over four hundred million land mines have been buried in eighty different countries; even with peace treaties, more than a hundred million unexploded mines remain in the ground today. Some devices—designed only to maim— injure more than seventy people a day, most of them children.

the mines, how would I deactivate them without getting myself killed? That's when Peter and I agreed to bring in the authorities. When Peter called the FBI office in Boston and mentioned potential violence, they insisted on meeting that afternoon.

"Do you think Gus is pretending to teach us enlightenment but is actually training us to be"—I could barely get out the next word—"terrorists? Maybe this is some kind of jihad?"

It took several moments before Peter answered. "I don't know about his politics, but I'd like to think Gus started off with good intentions. Unfortunately, everything so far tells me this was a scam from the beginning."

"But why here?" I asked. "Why plan violence in one of the most idyllic settings in the country?"

"I don't get it, either," Peter said. "Thoreau was the father of the nonviolence movement."

"That's it!" I ransacked my pack for the flyers I'd taken from the Concord Library. A yoga class, a writing workshop. I waved the blue page in Peter's face. "Because of its history, Walden is a favorite place for visiting dignitaries." I handed him the phone from the kitchen table.

"You better move up that appointment with the FBI," I said. "Next Thursday there's a panel on nonviolence at Walden with several VIPs from the Pentagon. I'll bet anything they're Gus's target."

Land mine

Janine was eager to tell the FBI agents everything. We told them about the survey maps, land mines, and Internet fund-raising. I also told them what the private investigator had uncovered about Gus. Both Peter and Janine were furious I hadn't shared that information before.

"I'm not sure if it makes a difference," Peter said, "but I think he's Middle Eastern."

"Iranian," Janine added.

"It doesn't matter if he's from Israel or Iceland," I said. "He's got land mines!"

The two agents sat back in their chairs; I thought they were going to congratulate Janine, Peter, and me on our outstanding citizenship. I was wrong.

"We did a background check on you before coming here today," the first one told me. "You ran for president last election, right?"

"Guilty as charged."

"And before that, didn't you fake your own death?"

I explained the circumstances of my disappearance, but neither agent seemed appeased.

"You created a situation for dramatic effect to suit your own purposes," the second agent said. "How do we know you're not doing that now?"

"This doesn't have anything to do with me. It's a matter of national security."

The first one cracked a slight smile and nodded to the other. "The boy who cried wolf."

"It's more like the boy who cried terrorism," I said. "No matter what happened in my past, doesn't this seem worth investigating?"

"You want to talk about the present—weren't you recently arrested at Walden Pond for resisting arrest and disregarding posted regulations? Weren't you responsible for a child getting mauled by a rabid dog?"

"He wasn't rabid!" Janine and I shouted.

I did my best to explain the Brady incident.[96] The second agent wrote down everything I said but was not impressed.

The first agent checked his notes. "If anyone's planning criminal activity at Walden, seems like you're the first person the FBI should investigate."

"I'm really a nice guy—I just donated a kidney to save someone's life."

"Good for you," the first said. "But we take terrorism seriously, just as seriously as we take false terrorism threats."

"There's nothing fake going on here," Peter said. "I'm a taxpayer—I insist you follow up on these leads."

Both men got up from the kitchen table. "I'm afraid you can't insist on anything, sir."

---

[96] It killed me to resurrect the whole story in front of Janine.

Since neither Peter nor I were having any luck, Janine tried pouring on the charm. She told the agents how Gus had tricked her into a relationship, how he was raising money by lying to people on the Internet. She made a credible, passionate case. They didn't buy it.

The first man turned squarely to face me. "We've read your 'sermons' and your presidential speeches. You're big on questioning authority, right? Well, it's my professional opinion that this is some kind of game to you, that you get a kick out of rocking the boat. We've got better things to do at the Federal Bureau of Investigation than follow up crazy leads by people trying to tear down democracy."

"Are you insane? I'm trying to *help*."

"We're not looking for help from people like you."

"I stand by my son," Peter said. "You're going to have a lot of explaining to do when your superiors find out you knew about this attack before it happened and did nothing to stop it."

The man paused in the doorway and turned slowly back around to face Peter. "Are you threatening us?"

"No, I just hope we're wrong and no lives are lost. But if there *is* an incident and it comes out that the FBI knew about it ahead of time . . ." Peter held up his hands in a shrug.

The two agents smirked. The first one motioned toward Peter, then to me. "Like father, like son. A family of troublemakers."

As I watched them walk to their unmarked car, I pointed to the taller man. "Glad our country's being protected by a guy who can't even figure out he's walking around with the price tag still on the waistband of his pants."

When the man turned back toward us, his cheeks flushed with embarrassment. He hurried to their car and drove away.

Janine was angry, but I almost felt relieved. My whole life, I've had to do things on my own. I spoke out against injustice, I got involved in politics, I tried to make myself a better person. No one had ever handed me a better world on a plate. If you want to change something, change it. Don't sit around and wait for someone else to do it because—guess what?—no one will. It was a motto I knew by heart.

"Forget the FBI," I said. "We know the players, we have access. We'll take care of this ourselves."

Peter adamantly disagreed. It was too dangerous, there was too much at stake. Ammunition was involved.

I listened politely and said, "Yes, I understand." But I knew what I had to do.

I sat in the dark of the cabin replica to think. Thoreau's mantra, "*Simplify, simplify,*" played endlessly in my head. I'd acted as straightforwardly as possible by calling the proper authorities but hadn't expected such a negative response. I knew I had to get to the heart of the matter and confront Gus. This strategy might be simple, but I dreaded it nonetheless.

I approached the makeshift tent Gus had erected deep in the woods. The place looked like command central for something imminent and evil. Laptops, boxes, flashlights, shovels, even racks of clothes filled the small space. A large pine table was covered with one of the survey maps. The map was held in place by a sizable bowie knife.

Gus entered right behind me, his face smudged with grease as if he were at war. "The prodigal son returns."

"Stop calling me son."

He folded his wide arms across his chest and asked what he could do for me.

"You can call off whatever it is you're planning."

He told me he'd never been much of a planner and was more the spontaneous type. I grabbed the survey map from the long table.

"You pretended we were surveying the land to walk in Thoreau's shoes, but what you're really up to is determining where to bury land mines."

Instead of denying it, his smile grew even wider. "Is that what you think?"

I told him yes.

"Well, since your thoughts manifest to actions, I'm sure there *will* be mines."

"Are you trying to blame this on *me*? I'm only thinking about them because of you!"

"You've got to learn to accept responsibility for your thoughts. I taught you that weeks ago."

I had to give the guy credit; it was amazing how he could turn an argument around. Behind him, Mike and several of the other guys suddenly appeared.

"Look out, boys," Gus said. "Larry here is thinking about terrorism so there *will* be terrorism. Someone should notify the authorities."

Mike grabbed me by the arm and threw me to the ground.

"What's wrong with you?" I shouted. "I just had surgery!"

As if in response to the word *surgery,* betagold entered the tent. She'd been sporting a polyester camouflage tracksuit and beret[97] since she'd moved into Victopia a few days ago.

"Take him outside and beat the crap out of him," she told Mike.

"Whoa, Che betagold!" I wiped off my jeans and stood up. "I didn't give you one of my major organs so you could become

---

[97] Where does she shop? Grandmas "R" Fanatics?

a revolutionary. You must have *some* gratitude for the sacrifice I made."

When she knocked me back down to the ground with her walking stick, I took that as a no.

"I refuse to have my kidney take part in any criminal activity," I added. "In fact, I've just decided I want it back. I'm going to see if we can have the operation reversed."

To my surprise, she took the bowie knife from the table and handed it to me. She removed the jacket of her tracksuit and turned around. "You want your kidney back?" betagold asked. "Take it."

Gus's impish smile made me think he might actually be enjoying this. Mike started to go for the knife, but Gus held him back.

"Go ahead, Larry. If that's what you want, do it. I'll even hold her down for you." He held betagold against the long table.

I didn't want to remove her kidney—certainly not without anesthesia or sterile equipment—but what *did* I want to do? I thought about holding the knife to betagold's throat and using her as a hostage to leave the tent alive. I could defend myself against Mike and his gang of spiritual thugs all the way to the parking lot, but that also seemed extreme. In the end, I threw the knife on the table like a bartender whipping a bottle of beer down the length of the bar.

"I don't want any trouble," I said. "But if something illegal is going on, it stops now."

"Oh, really?" Mike picked up the knife from the table. "And why should we care what you think?"

"Because I told the FBI everything—about the survey

141

maps, the land mines, the visiting dignitaries from the Pentagon on Thursday. They've got this place under surveillance. You're all looking at serious jail time."

I watched fear spread across Mike's face like a cumulonimbus cloud.[98] He and the others turned to Gus, who didn't seem fazed in the least.

"You told the FBI, and they didn't believe you, probably because of your past shenanigans. The fact that you're here right now tells me they didn't."

Why was this guy always right?

"I don't want innocent people getting hurt," I said.

"No one from the Pentagon is innocent!" For the first time, Gus lost his cool and started screaming. "The war machine is out of control! When does it end? People like us"—he motioned to everyone in the tent, including me—"need to put our foot down and stop the madness!"

"Not with more madness," I said. "You'll only make things worse. And using Thoreau and Gandhi as cover-ups, that's just plain wrong." I kept telling myself the P.I. had called back to say there'd been a mistake, that Gus wasn't my biological father. But part of me recalled Peter's description of him as a paranoid rabble-rouser. I'd always wanted to meet my father. But I hardly wanted him to be ranting in a tent about anarchy.

I thought I was getting through to Mike; he was digging a small hole with the toe of his sneaker, avoiding Gus's gaze. But I was mistaken. After a moment, Mike looked up at me with

---

[98] If you've never seen one in real life, you should do a Google image search. They're pretty amazing.

even more determination. "We've been working too hard for one goody-two-shoes to screw it up. You think you're so special—it makes me sick. As if making the world a better place is an actual career path and you're bucking for a promotion. Who are you trying to impress, anyway?"

I was just about to answer when his fist nailed my side. I tried to protect my one good kidney as he came in for another punch. I fell to the ground with the sound of betagold and Gus cheering him on.

I woke up nursing my kidney, but it gratefully seemed oblivious to yesterday's fight. I rolled back the bandage to gaze at the scar. Pink, raised, and amazingly only three inches long. Yesterday it seemed like a merit badge for Selfless Service to Mankind. Today it signified nothing more than a foolish decision.

When Beth entered my room, she noticed the sticky notes covering the wall above my desk. "This reminds me of when you decided to run for president. You used so many stickies, it looked like you'd re-wallpapered the room in yellow."

I leaned back in the swivel chair and tried to make sense of all the information. "There's something else going on, but I don't know what. Images that don't make sense, scraps of conversation, and those chess pieces—it's almost as if this is some kind of game. Sometimes I feel as if Gus set up this whole thing for my benefit."

"He's planning to attack some bigwigs from the Pentagon and it's about *you*? Even on the Swensen narcissistic-meter, that theory's off the charts."

I had no evidence, no proof that Gus was playing me for a fool; it was just a growing feeling of unease. "There was a rack of clothes in Gus's tent, some of them still with price tags. The

FBI agent who came to the house had a price tag hanging from the waistband of his pants. Coincidence, sure, but what if Gus is orchestrating some huge 'Josh' game?"

"Your self-absorption is killing me!"

"Secret phone calls, a guy with a videocamera I keep bumping into at the pond, and when I was talking to Katie the other day, she kept checking her hand as if she was reading crib notes. Everything related to Gus seems staged. It's like he's a puppetmaster, pulling strings to make the rest of us dance."

"Why don't you try and turn him in again?"

I told her I'd visited the park ranger who'd arrested me with Brady, thinking he might be interested in the violent act being planned on his precious historic site. Maybe he would've listened if someone else had brought him the information, but all he saw when he looked at me was trouble. He barely glanced up from his newspaper as he told me to get lost.

"Well, we've got to do something," Beth said. "The dignitaries will be here in less than a week."

I pointed to the wall of scribbled notes and told her I'd contacted several organizations specializing in deactivating land mines. Unfortunately many of them were located in other parts of the world. "There's a man in Cambodia who can get here in two weeks, but that's too late."

Beth climbed onto my bed as I explained what I'd learned in the past few days. I told her about the trained dogs who sniffed out explosives. Sadly, the cost was prohibitive.

"Too bad you got Brady killed," Beth said. "Maybe he could've pulled a Lassie and saved the day."

I grabbed one of my sneakers from the floor and hurled it at her. She threw it back with equal velocity and nearly nailed my head. As I got up to tackle her, I noticed Peter in the doorway. He asked Beth if he could talk to me privately; on her way out of the room, she sailed the other sneaker at me, clocking me on the ear.

Peter surveyed the wall of notes. "I see you're back to your old self—making plans, taking action—all the stuff you're good at." He handed me a piece of paper, which I recognized as the letter from the DNA testing service I was sure I'd thrown away at the hospital. "So you think your biological father is still alive?"

"Not anymore. Once I saw 'Inconclusive Results' on that letter, I put that lamebrain idea out of my head forever."[99]

"You think someone is your biological father, you go to the trouble of sending DNA to a lab, and you don't tell me about it?"

"I didn't want to hurt you."

"I thought our relationship was a little more honest than that."

Before I had a chance to explain, Peter jumped back in. "Let's see—you pretend to kill yourself, put me through unparalleled grief, then come waltzing into my life as if nothing happened. I take you back with open arms. You run for national office, I'm with you every step of the way. You take off for eight months after your girlfriend, send me depressing letters from the road, then come back and never leave the couch, not even

---

[99] A bald-faced lie. I'd tried to obtain other samples from Gus—used tissues, bloody Band-Aids—but every time I came close to grabbing one, another student mysteriously appeared. It was only a matter of time before I'd succeed in acquiring a good sample.

to eat or take a shower. You need money for some cockamamie enlightenment course, and I give it to you. But this"—he held out the letter again—"this is too much. You want to find another father so badly, you have my permission. Go find one."

I followed him down the hall, apologizing with every step. "It was stupid. I should've told you. I don't want another father—I have you."

When he turned around to face me, he looked as if he'd aged ten years since yesterday. "Just tell me you didn't think it was Gus. That's all I want to know."

Tell someone what he wants to hear or be honest? It seemed like the eternal unanswerable question. I opted for honesty and told him yes. He gave me a slow, sad smile.

"Your mother left me with a handful, that's for sure. If someone told me back when I proposed that I'd end up here, I would've taken that sapphire ring off her finger, turned around, and run."

His words hit me like the frigid water at Walden. "Gus isn't my father, *you* are. I was just telling Beth this is all a game to him, that he's intentionally messing with me. I don't even know what's real anymore."

Peter put his hand on my shoulder. "Let me make this easy for you. You're welcome to stay till after the holidays, until college starts in January. After that? I'm done."

"But I don't want—"

He held up his hand to stop me. "I'm too old for this, Josh. Too old for FBI agents, presidential debates, fake suicides, and land mines. I just want to run my little business in peace. Is that asking too much for a guy my age?"

I had to agree it wasn't. I told him I'd take care of everything myself[100] and would be on a train to Princeton in less than a month. When I looked at him leaning against the table, I couldn't decide which wore Peter out more, the lethargic, depressed Josh or the hyperactive, solve-the-world's-problems-by-dinnertime version. But I knew one thing—neither would be Peter's problem anymore. I was now officially on my own.

---

[100] Don't ask me how because I don't know.

PART FOUR

"We either make ourselves miserable,
or we make ourselves strong.
The amount of work is the same."

Carlos Castaneda

Needless to say, Christmas was a disaster. I almost would've preferred an all-out brawl; the silent, polite day Peter and I shared reeked of phony cheer. I was relieved when he excused himself to work on pitching his event-planning services to a new client in Framingham.

Beth and I exchanged Christmas presents according to the rule we'd instituted several years ago—homemade gifts only. In between searching online for ways to deactivate land mines, I gathered up dryer lint, blended it with water and scraps of colored paper, then pressed the mushy pulp into a large plastic container. After much drying and experimentation, I ended up with several sheets of beautiful, thick, homemade paper. She loved it.

For my gift, Beth had woven together strips of brown and black suede to form a chessboard you could fold into your pocket. I tucked it into the collar of my shirt. "A checkered ascot."

She grabbed it and placed it on top of her head. "A multicolored yarmulke."

I took it back and pretended to blow my nose. "A handkerchief."

We went back and forth with the joke for much too long, as we did every year.

"Seriously," Beth said. "You've been so obsessed with Gus, I figured you could put this to good use."

I retrieved the chess pieces Gus had given me and placed them on the new board. When I finished, I looked up to see Beth putting on her coat.

"I've got so much work to do," she said.

"It's Christmas!"

"Unless someone left psych and poli sci papers under the tree, I've got to go." She kissed me on the top of my head.

Sitting alone with a partly finished chess game seemed an apt metaphor for my life. Instead of playing solo, I borrowed Peter's car to find Janine. She snuck out of Victopia as if her father was asleep upstairs.

"How come I can't come in?" I asked yet again.

"Katie's parents are here for the day—I just want to give her some privacy." She hopped in Peter's car and we drove to Walden.

The fresh snow nestled on the pines made the reservation seem as if it too had been decorated for the holidays. Janine and I sat on the stone wall down by the beach and breathed in the cold air, watching it escape from our mouths moments later as vapor.

"I searched Gus's room yesterday while he was out—no boxes or canisters resembling the ones you found in his truck."

"I know I didn't imagine them," I said. "We should check his tent. I doubt anyone will be there Christmas Day."

We gathered our courage and hiked into the woods. Like

extras in a war movie, we inched along the ground as we approached Gus's headquarters, finally making our way inside. Lots of camouflage gear and lanterns but no land mines.

"Let's find the maps," I suggested. "At least we'll know where the mines are buried."

We tore apart the tent until we found a cache of rolled-up maps. Unfortunately, they were our original versions, without the critical *x*'s. Janine tossed them to the floor in a tirade of curses.[101]

I couldn't help but think of the conversation I'd had with Beth about Gus. Why did I still get the impression he was up to something more than terrorism? Some kind of sick game? As if to illustrate the point, I spotted a carved king on the pine table. I shoved it into my pocket. When I'd been here last, one of the survey maps had been fastened to the table by the bowie knife. I ran my hand across the tabletop, and sure enough, the impressions of several *x*'s were carved into the soft wood. I grabbed one of the maps and laid it over the table. Janine caught on to what I was doing and put on one of the miner helmets from the shelf. When I pressed down on the map and she shone the light, we could faintly make out where the *x*'s had been drawn.

"It's not this map," I said. "The *x*'s are in the middle of the pond."

We tried four more maps until we found one where the *x*'s corresponded to places people would walk. I marked the *x*'s with a pencil, then rolled the map under my arm.

---

[101] A far cry from the enlightened girl I found here weeks ago. It's amazing what killing a girl's dog will do.

153

"Finding the locations of the mines is the best Christmas present I could've asked for," I said. "Let's go dig them up."

"Are you nuts?" Janine yelled. "We're not trained for that."

"The biggest problem in digging up mines is that you don't know where they're buried," I explained. "But now we know exactly where they are. Professionals just use garden trowels— the excavation part isn't that hard."

"Are you listening to yourself? We're not digging up land mines!"

"What else am I supposed to do? I've contacted the FBI, and they don't believe me. I've got to put my money where my mouth is. It's the most tangible lesson Gus taught us."

She pulled out her cell phone. "I'm telling Peter you've finally lost it."

I grabbed the phone from her hand. "I'm not Peter's problem anymore—he's made that clear. I'll take care of this myself."

"I want nothing to do with this." Janine stormed out of the tent but returned a moment later. She tossed me the miner's helmet. "Merry Christmas. If you're going to kill yourself for real this time, you might want to see what you're doing."

I spent the next several days digging and avoiding park rangers, but the most hazardous thing I found was a rusty trial-size can of hairspray. I used my mother's old gardening tools for good luck. The meticulously detailed instructions I'd downloaded from the Internet reminded people to use the utmost care even after numerous failed attempts. I went so far as to borrow a metal detector from Mr. Cullen down the street.[102] But instead of making my job easier, the metal detector added hours to each hole, forcing me to dig for things like bottlecaps and penknives. I was beginning to think the entire plan was a hallucination. Maybe I'd never seen those canisters at all.

Betagold knew I was up to something; she happened to hike by the area several times a day. Mike and the others seemed too busy with Gus's regimen to pay me any notice. As I slowly brushed away the dirt from a small hole on the western shore of the pond, betagold pulled up a log.

"I hope you're not holding any grudges about last week."

---

[102] He uses it to locate things people lost on the beach at Castle Hill. Once he found a diamond ring from the '40s that he gave his wife for their anniversary. I'm not sure how Mrs. Cullen felt, but I love that kind of recycling.

I told her to get lost.

"I felt remorse afterward, I really did," betagold said. "Part of you is inside me, after all."

"Don't remind me. Stupidest thing I ever did was save your life." I suddenly realized that betagold hadn't watched where she was walking when she'd approached me. Since the transplant, she'd been on Gus's A-list. If there were land mines buried here, she wouldn't be walking around so casually.

I threw down the trowel and sat cross-legged beside her. "So if the mines aren't here, where are they?"

She played dumb[103] and told me she didn't know what I was talking about.

"Gus told Janine all about them," I lied. "About the dignitaries on Thursday. About making a statement to the Pentagon."

I watched her expression as she tried to decide if I really had any information.

"The bigwigs," I continued. "The survey maps, the mines—Janine's been in on the plan since the get-go."

"I thought we weren't supposed to tell you anything, in case you tried to get all heroic again."

"Me?" I motioned to her back. "I've already done my one good deed for this year, thank you very much."

Betagold still eyed me cautiously. "If Gus told Janine everything, then she knows where they are and I don't have to tell you.[104] Besides, if they're using antihandling devices along with the mines, you won't be able to just dig them up anyway."

---

[103] Or was she just *pretending* to?

[104] A flaw in my logic, unfortunately.

156

Betagold had obviously been paying attention to Gus's work. But now she seemed a bit worried as she pointed toward his tent. "I'd follow Gus to the ends of the earth since he found me a donor,[105] but these past few days he's acting like it's a full moon day and night."

I made another attempt at obtaining privileged information. "He's probably got a lot on his mind, making sure everything goes off as planned on Thursday."

"He's the opposite of worried—that's what has me scared."

I gathered up the gardening tools and hiked toward Gus's tent to see for myself.

Several disciples stood like zombies guarding the hillside. Were they on something? I wondered if my theory was wrong and they were victims, not accomplices, in Gus's plan. Like a modern-day Jim Jones,[106] maybe he was planning something dangerous for his followers. I ran up the hill at a faster clip.

Inside the tent, the scene was just as disturbing. Even with the end-of-December weather, Gus wore his patched denim cutoffs with no shirt. His belly was painted in vibrant colors in a psychedelic pattern with words like *Kablam!* and *Pow!* scrawled above each nipple.[107] His face was painted gold with thick black outlines around his eyes, nose, and mouth. A white towel was wrapped around his head. The makeshift turban and long gray beard added to the unsettling image. Fronds of

---

[105] Yes, betagold, that would be me.

[106] A cult leader in Guyana who led his followers in a mass suicide by spiking their drinks with cyanide—913 people died.

[107] The onomatopoeic words reminded me of the old *Batman* show I'd been addicted to on TV Land. That was only a few months ago, yet seemed like years.

rhododendron and holly were stacked around his chair as if it were a throne. He carried a six-pack of beer.

"What the hell is going on?" I asked.

"'In Wildness is the preservation of the World.'"

"I doubt Thoreau was talking about getting trashed and planning terrorism."

Gus punched a hole in the bottom of a beer can, popped the top, then tipped his head back and shot the beer in one gulp.

"The new year is upon us." He wiped his mouth with the back of his hand. "Not just literally but figuratively. A time to be reborn, a time to start anew."

"Enough already. I just want you to be honest with me."

"Like you were honest with Peter about looking for your biological father?"

How does this man know everything?

I decided Gus might be bluffing and tried to stay focused, difficult as that might be.

As Gus observed the tranced-out disciples, I knew where I'd seen this place before—in my imagination back in high school when we read Joseph Conrad's *Heart of Darkness.* The book had given me the creeps for weeks, and the thought that I might be re-enacting it now sent a round of goose bumps up both arms. The only things missing from the scene were decapitated heads stuck on poles.[108]

I tried to access my brain's hard drive to remember the book. Was I supposed to be Marlow to Gus's Kurtz? Was I

---

[108] No Brady references, please.

meant to capture or kill him? The only thing possibly worse than a national historic site with land mines was a frightening fictional character coming to life in some pseudo-Congo setting whispering "The horror! The horror!" I had to get out quick.

"Oh, come on," Gus said. "It's the end of the world, anyway—don't take yourself so seriously."

"Me?" I pointed to the interior design of his fort. "Don't you think you're being too realistic with this idolatry thing?"

"Real? What is real?" he asked. "Have you figured that one out yet? Make sure you get back to me when you do."

As I hurried back down the hill, I realized the teacher I'd invested so much time and effort in was as clueless about reality as I was.

Janine jumped on my bed while I was still asleep.

"Peter let me in. You have to get up." She took my jeans and sweatshirt from the floor and threw them at me. "It's all a game. Gus is screwing with us."

I sat up, leaning on my elbows. A girl was in my room.[109]

"*Wake up,*" Janine said. "You were right."

"About what?"

She sat on the edge of the bed, as far away from me as she could get.[110] "Because I was in on it."

"What?"

"Pretending to have an affair with him, planting those fake land mines in his truck—"

Although I'd had only a few hours of sleep, Janine now had my full attention. "Gus was messing around with my mind, and you were *helping* him? Is that what you're saying?"

"Don't be mad. Gus was trying to teach you about the nature of reality. He told me if I cared about you, I should help

---

[109] Finally!

[110] The usual reaction girls have.

him. That you had a great sense of humor and would totally appreciate the cosmic joke."

Even though I was wearing the lame candy-cane boxers Peter had given me last week, I jumped out of bed and paced around the room. "Let me get this straight. I've spent hundreds of hours doing research on land mines, I contacted the FBI, I dug thirty holes around Walden Pond, *I GAVE UP MY KIDNEY TO GET YOU OUT OF GUS'S CLUTCHES*, and now you tell me you were in cahoots with him all along? Is this your idea of a joke?"

She stood up and faced me head-on. "So I guess we're even for Brady."

"Is that what this is about?"

She headed toward the door without a trace of remorse. "Brady, plus thinking I betrayed you on the campaign. I'm sure that played into it too." She waved goodbye without looking at me. "Nice shorts, by the way."

I dialed Beth ten times until she finally picked up. I told her everything Janine had just told me.

"I hate it when people play devil's advocate," she finally said, "but what if Gus is screwing with you *now*? What if he's using Janine to tell you there are no land mines when there really are?"

"Don't you think my Rube Goldberg mind hasn't thought of that? Suppose she's really innocent—"

"Let's not go that far."

"Suppose she's really innocent," I repeated, "and he's talked her into thinking she's doing me a favor by saying there are no land mines."

"Or she's still pissed about her dog and was happy to send you off on a wild-goose chase. What does Peter say?"

I couldn't admit that Peter and I had barely spoken. I knew Beth would go ballistic with the next question, but I asked it anyway. "Suppose he *is* my biological father. Why is he torturing me? Is this some kind of test?"

"For the last time, he's not your father! What are the chances?" She interrupted her rant to ask if I was near a TV. "There's a crawl on CNN saying the Secretary of Defense and the other Pentagon guys had to cancel their appearances in Boston for some emergency meeting back in D.C."

I raced to the living room to verify Beth's story. "So, that's it. We're done. If there are land mines—and who even knows what to believe anymore?—their targets are no longer in town. So we're free."

"Take the train to Providence," Beth said. "We're on break, but there's a huge party tonight. Let's celebrate."

I asked her what she was talking about.

"Hel-lo! It's New Year's Eve, did you forget?"

I'd been so busy trying to stay one step ahead of Gus that I'd totally forgotten what day it was. Beth invited me to come down again and was disappointed when I told her no.

"Just tell me why," she said. "As if I don't know what you're going to say."

I tried to explain that even though the land mines might've been fakes and even though the Pentagon guys weren't coming, there was still a slight chance that Janine was lying and Gus *had* planted the ammunition.

162

"But the big photo op got canceled! There's no one to blow up."

"Except for tourists, and hikers, and Thoreau freaks like me. I can't go to a party when there's even a chance Gus might've been serious."

"What does Superman do now that everyone uses cell phones and there aren't any more phone booths?" Beth asked. "Where do you change into your leotard and cape?"

I told her I'd talk to her next year[111] and grabbed Peter's keys from the counter. I threw my sleeping bag into the car and headed to Walden.

---

[111] I've been using that joke since I was five.

If I hadn't been worried about the apocalypse, the moment might've been perfect. The full moon looked as if it had been run through Photoshop; it was five times its normal size. The night was not too cold, with barely any wind. I stood at the top of my favorite ridge and took a mental picture of the reflection of the moon and trees on the pond, an image to call up when I needed something tranquil and right just the way it was.

I spent the next hour walking through the woods searching for trip wires or freshly dug holes. After a while, I realized Janine had probably been telling me the truth when she said the whole land-mine thing had been a setup. Until I saw a flyer taped to one of the trees advertising a midnight peace vigil on the south end of the pond, I'd totally forgotten[112] we were on the cusp of a new year.

I unzipped my sleeping bag and wrapped it around me. These past few months, I'd walked in the footsteps of Thoreau and performed craftwork in the spirit of Gandhi. Had emulating these icons of nonviolence and simplicity rubbed off on me at all? Maybe it was a waste of time for each generation to reinvent

---

[112] Again.

the wheel. Maybe there were people who lived dozens or hundreds of years earlier who had the game of life figured out. Maybe all we had to do was follow their lead with a few tweaks of our own. I played a game of What Would Thoreau Do and realized that, although his life was simple, it was full and varied. I doubted he'd waste time trying to figure out Gus. He had beans to harvest, wood to chop. I had to get on with my life.

I fell asleep tucked between the earth and the stars.

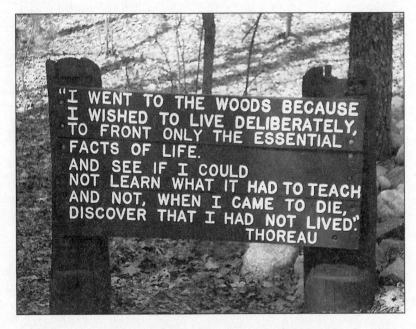

Quote from *Walden* at the cabin site

I woke up half an hour later to the sound of Gus's voice. He wore camouflage cutoffs and a sleeveless fleece vest with no shirt underneath. A smudge of leftover gold paint remained on his neck like a neon hickey. He leaned back on the earth beside me.

"I'm hitting the road," he said. "But I wanted to say goodbye."

I asked him why he was leaving.

"I'm a nomad—I no mad at you, you no mad at me."

I had to smile at the lameness of the joke. I asked him where he was going and what would happen to his disciples. He told me he had no planned destination and his students were ready to practice without him. When I sat up to talk, I noticed a large group of people at the opposite end of the pond, probably the peace activists preparing for their midnight vigil.

Gus propped himself up on one elbow and wondered if there was anything I wanted to ask him. Here was a chance to finally make the inconclusive results of the DNA test conclusive. But I first chose to ask about something more pressing. "Were there ever any land mines?"

He shook his head and laughed. "Were you looking in my truck? Those weren't land mines."

The wave of relief I felt was physical.

"You must've been worried out of your mind," he said.

"Petrified."

He laughed again. "No, those were bombs. They look like land mines, but different results, believe me."

"Did you say *bombs*?"

"Your pal betagold was chomping at the bit for this assignment. You'd think with a new kidney she'd be eager for a few more years of life, but when she makes up her mind, watch out."

I begged him to explain.

"She wants to sacrifice herself for a worthy cause."

"What worthy cause? Is this part of that game Janine was talking about? Are you putting me on? Tell me!"

"Betagold has really embraced the dark side. I gotta say, she's one of my most committed students."

My kidney was giving betagold the strength to kill innocent people? What happened to enjoying another few years with her grandchildren? I tried to piece together the disparate scraps of information, but one thing didn't make sense. "The Pentagon canceled. What's the point?"

Gus looked confused. "Those guys from the Defense Department? What do they have to do with anything?"

"Weren't they your targets?"

A huge grin spread across his face. "That's so *obvious*! If you want to put the fun back in fundamentalism, you've got to do something people aren't expecting."[113]

---

[113] I don't know about the fun in fundamentalism, but Gus certainly had the mental down.

What had I missed? I asked him again who the target was.

He nodded toward the group on the other side of the pond. "You know who I hate more than those thieves at the Pentagon? Activists who are so disorganized the best they can do is hold up candles and hope for peace. Activism used to mean bringing a government to its knees—standing for hours in the rain, walking to work for months rather than breaking a bus boycott, chaining yourself to a tank. People today think they're doing something by complaining to their friends about how much things suck. It makes me sick. We stopped a war during my lifetime. Now the government runs rampant over our civil rights, and no one wants to get off the couch except to hold a candle." He waved his arm across the pond as if he were a magician. "As soon as it turns midnight, betagold and your new kidney are blowing those do-gooders into a thousand picket sign–holding pieces."

This had to be a joke. What kind of twisted mind blows up people praying for peace? But when I looked over at Gus, he made Conrad's Kurtz seem like Little Bo Peep. Between the glow of the moon and his wicked eyes, he appeared to be the devil himself.

"The beautiful thing is when they investigate afterward, your DNA is all over the diagrams and detonators," Gus said. "I saved enough of your blood sample to splatter on the evidence and pin tonight's terrorism on you. You were trying to get my DNA, but I got yours—different reasons, of course. And after your tête-à-tête with the FBI, it sounds like they'll be eager to buy my manufactured version of reality." He put his arm on my shoulder. "Goodbye, son. May the forest be with you."

I shoved him off me and sprinted down the hill.

Running along a narrow path through the woods at night is tricky, even with a full moon. I fell several times, once on my side, which had me clutching my solitary kidney in pain. I wished the pond were frozen so I could run across the ice to save time. It wasn't fear of the FBI or Gus's betrayal that propelled me forward but a passionate sense of purpose I hadn't felt in a long time. Sure, I'd made sacrifices—I'd given betagold enough life energy to let her implement her terrorist beliefs—but this was something else. Gus's violent plans were screwing with *my* world, and that was a whole different thing. Let the old guy wax nostalgic all he wanted, but messing with the future of my universe was not okay. As jumbled and confusing as these past months had been, I now realized I couldn't give up the struggle to make the world a better place. There was no one else to do it. Not because I was special—we were all equal to the task—but because I *wanted* to. The world was full of all this breathing, all these pumping hearts, all these ideas, all this *life*. It was time for people who chose not to positively contribute to get out of the way and let the rest of us give it a go.

I'd always had more questions than answers, and asking why seemed a giant waste of time. As okay as it was to accept reality, it was also perfectly right to try and change it. And that's what I was doing. I needed to stop waiting to be fixed; all I could do was start where I was. I was human and flawed. For the first time in my life, I felt like I actually belonged. Sitting and waiting around for burned-out adults like Gus to solve the world's problems seemed a surefire formula for failure. I ran through the darkness like a leopard chasing prey, picking up speed with every step.

Out of the corner of my eye, I caught a glimpse of the two giant koi reflected by the full moon. I hadn't seen them in several weeks, but as I ran by, their orange-and-white blur gave me hope. If they represented liberation, maybe I was finally free.

As I reached the edge of the clearing, I knocked over a man in a tie-dyed parka. I helped him up and asked him if he'd seen a grandmotherly type in a heavy vest.

"Are the Grannies for Peace here? I love them!"

I tried to place the man's face but couldn't. I gave up and ran from person to person in search of betagold. The moon, candles, music, and dancing combined to make the setting seem like a surrealist's dream. I wondered if I'd really just had a conversation with Gus or if I was still sleeping in my down bag on the other side of the pond. I actually looked across the water to see if my body was still there. I put my hands on my knees and caught my breath. Maybe this was an innocent group of people supporting peace and Gus was screwing with me again. But just as I considered abandoning the whole project, I realized where I'd seen the man with the parka—he was one of the agents from the FBI. Was it typical for federal agents to attend midnight peace rallies? Was he some kind of spy? If the FBI didn't believe me, why were they here now? I tore through the crowd to find him, and as I did, more and more people looked familiar. One man resembled one of the cops who'd arrested me. My perception of what was real and what wasn't totally blew apart. Was this all taking place in my mind? Was I having an official nervous breakdown?

Just as I was ready to fall down the well-known rabbit hole, I spotted betagold. She wore her black beret and camouflage tracksuit with a backpack strapped to her chest the way some people carry babies. She was walking straight into the center of the protestors.

"Stop!" I yelled. "Somebody grab her!"

It must've been close to midnight because the group started counting down. "Ten, nine, eight . . ."

"Somebody stop that woman!"

". . . seven, six, five . . ."

There were probably fifty people there, even a few small children. I didn't think twice about what I had to do. It wasn't my own life that flashed before my eyes as I raced to betagold; it was Gandhi's. I remembered an anecdote of a reporter running beside Gandhi's train to ask for a message to take back to his people. It was Gandhi's day of silence, so he scrawled a reply and handed the man a note. "My life is my message." That was what I thought of as I tried to save the others from betagold's bomb—not of Peter, Beth, Janine, or even joining my mom in the afterlife—just a poignant anecdote about someone else's time on this earth. But I guess if you have to have someone's life flash before your eyes, Gandhi's isn't a bad choice. In the seconds of slowed-down time, I realized my

172

life, too, was my message. I thought of the Thoreau quote, "If I am not I, who will be?" I finally understood the meaning of my life—to fully embrace being *me*—but unfortunately that life was now over. The irony made me laugh out loud as I threw myself on top of betagold.

"... four, three, two, one ..."

The explosion was deafening.

When Robert Oppenheimer described his reaction to seeing the first atomic bomb he'd developed light up the sky, he quoted from the Hindu scripture, the Bhagavad Gita.[114] "Now I am become death, the destroyer of worlds." But there wasn't a mushroom cloud at Walden that night; the sky was ablaze in red and green. I wasn't dead but very much alive, underneath a giant fireworks display. Several people shouted "Happy New Year!"

"Would you mind getting off me?" betagold asked. "You're hurting my leg."

I slowly rolled off her, still unsure about what was going on. "But I thought . . ." I pointed to the pack strapped across her chest.

She unzipped the bag, took out a bottle of champagne, and handed it to me with a smile. With the fireworks, the whole scene still appeared dreamlike—every person seemed familiar in some vague way. I felt as if several switches in my brain had been flipped.

Katie jumped me from behind. "So, what do you think?"

---

[114] Both Thoreau and Gandhi were huge fans of the text.

174

I asked her what she was talking about.

She didn't answer, just kissed me on the cheek and grabbed the bottle of champagne. "I'll e-mail you the photos of you digging for land mines. The earnest look on your face is priceless!"

Mike tackled me and apologized for being such a jerk. "I was just following the script, dude. No hard feelings?"

"Just tell me where Gus is."

Mike pointed down toward the pond.

On my way to find our leader, I ran smack into Janine. She wore a sequined dress, Cleopatra eyeliner, and platform shoes. It was the first time she'd worn "normal" Janine clothes since she'd been here.

"When you confessed to being part of Gus's plan the other morning, was that part of the game too?" I asked.

"Everything was scripted," she said. "There were very few improvisations."

I felt something rub against my leg and looked down to find Brady, head and all. I nearly fell to the ground in relief. "YOU PRETENDED YOUR DOG WAS DEAD?"

"It was incredibly hard, believe me. I actually had nightmares. Every time you showed up at Victopia unannounced, you thought I was with Gus, but I was hiding Brady."

"What are you, a Method actor? What about his ashes?"

"I took them from your fireplace." Janine gave betagold a high-five when she approached.[115]

---

[115] WHAT IS HAPPENING TO MY WORLD?

"Tracy did a really great job too, don't you think?" Janine asked.

"I used to do community theater years ago," betagold added. "This was so much fun." She gave me a playful nudge. "Screwing around with your head was just an added benefit."

"WHAT ABOUT MY KIDNEY?" I said. "I wish someone had let me in on the joke before I went under the knife."

Janine covered her mouth and laughed. "About that kidney—"

"What?"

She and betagold exchanged glances.

"You don't mean . . ." I reached underneath my shirt. "I have a scar to prove it."

"The guy who designed your scar apprenticed with the makeup whiz who did *The Nutty Professor*," Janine said.

Betagold joined in Janine's laughter.

I pointed to the space separating betagold and me. "So there was no . . ."

Janine continued to laugh.

"There's no way Mass General was in on this," I said.

"That's a funny story," Janine said. "You'll have to ask the puppetmaster about it."

"So the pains, the recovery—that was all in my head?"

"You never had more than that Valium," Janine answered. "In a real organ donation, you would've had to undergo more rigorous screenings."

"I've got to give you credit," betagold said. "I would've let you die before I gave up anything that valuable to you. You really surprised me with your generosity."

176

I didn't have my kidney removed? I borrowed Janine's cell and called Beth. Between the party noises here and in Providence, I could barely make out a word she said.

"Gus has been twisting and manipulating my life all along."

Beth laughed until I told her about Brady and the fake transplant.[116] "You could sue him!" she said. "I've never heard of such a violation!"

She told me she'd find a quiet place to talk and to call her back. On my way to a calmer place on the hill, I finally spotted Gus. He was talking to two young women in togas and ski jackets. It took a few moments to recall where I'd seen them—the makeup department at Bloomingdale's.

So my mother never told me to study with Gus? She still hadn't spoken to me? Could the news get any worse?

As I approached Gus, I noticed other people out of context—the guy with the videocamera, Peter's ex-wife Katherine, and Marlene from Bloomingdale's. How wide had Gus cast his net for this little game?

Gus wore a Viking hat with two large horns and was blowing into a noisemaker. As he excused himself from the girls, I held myself back from punching him in the gut.

"So the dog was a lie, the transplant was a lie—what else?"

He shrugged. "The arrest with the park rangers, getting rejected from Princeton, the land mines, the FBI agents, selling the paint-by-numbers on eBay." He blew the noisemaker into my face. "Everything was a lie. I told you the first day we met

---

[116] Gus was right about one thing, though—the power of the mind. I could've sworn I'd felt pain after the surgery.

that life was a game." He reached into his pocket and handed me a pawn—a perfect metaphor for how I felt.

I forced myself to ask the next question. "What about the inconclusive results on the DNA test? If there's any bit of truth I can squeeze out of you, can you at least be honest about that?"

He tucked the noisemaker into the pocket of his overalls. "I'm not your father," Gus said. "But I'd be proud if I were." He reached out to hug me, but I turned away.

"You've been jerking me around for months," I said.

"Are you any more awake?"

Although the scene around me seemed like a carnival taking place in my unconscious, I had to admit I did feel more alive. I reluctantly congratulated Gus on his meticulous orchestration.

Gus looked confused. "Me? I'm just another actor. I was told to show up, and I did."

"What are you talking about? Then who . . ."

He pointed a few yards away to someone wearing a pointy wizard hat and a long purple cloak. I moved through the crowd until I was right behind the small group. The hat looked like one I'd owned years ago; I recognized the crooked moons and stars. I spun the wizard around, eager to see the person who'd manipulated every facet of my life for the past two months.

"I thought you were going to call me back." Beth held up the cell phone buried in her giant sleeve. She gave me a huge kiss. "Happy New Year, Josh."

PART FIVE

"We shall not cease from exploration,
And the end of all our exploring
Will be to arrive where we started
And know the place for the first time."

T. S. Eliot
"Four Quartets"

"YOU?"

I dragged Beth down the path to a more secluded part of the park. She was so elated, she bounced with every step. I told her to tell me everything.

"First, just tell me you liked it," she said. "I'd die if I thought you were angry."

"Of course I'm angry! You completely altered my definitions of real and not real."

"That's the good news," she said. "But what are you mad about?"

Where to begin? I ticked off the giant list of grievances and humiliations I'd suffered in the past few months. Not only had they been avoidable, they were premeditated. Beth listened so intently I thought she might reach into her cloak, pull out her laptop, and start taking notes.

"But what did you think of the performances? The drama club at school was great, and I found a lot of people on craigslist. I tried to get course credit for this as an independent project, but my department head turned me down."

I asked her to tell me about Gus.

181

"Big Patriots fan. I met him while I was getting new tires put on my father's car."

"What?"

"He's a part-time vet tech in Foxboro. Really nice guy."

"I've been getting spiritual advice from someone who weighs dogs at an animal clinic?"

"I thought he did a great job. Just goes to show you—people you meet every day are perfectly capable of helping you on your path."

I felt a swath of redness move across my face. Was I so desperate for advice that I glommed onto anyone for guidance? "And the hospital?"

"The operation"—she held up her fingers in quotes, a habit I've always hated—"took place in an OR, just not at Mass General."

"I'm afraid to ask."

"The operating room at Gus's vet's office."

"Are you kidding?"

"Why not? The people in scrubs were professionals, just for animals. When Gus asked them if we could use the space, they said yes right away."

"I thought I heard barking! Where did I recuperate—and don't tell me a kennel."

Beth jumped up and down with laughter. She was really having fun with this.

"The Holiday Inn in Dedham. We got a room for three days, brought in a hospital bed, IV, and monitors we rented from a medical supply store."

"And the nurses?"

"Luckily, you didn't need any medical care. Those people were all looking for extra cash on craigslist. Closest anyone came to medical experience was the guy who worked at the piercing booth at the mall."

I asked about the scar.

"My sister's friend Kyle did a great job, right? You need special remover to take it off. I wanted you to get a real tattoo of a scar so you'd have something to remember this whole thing by, but Janine talked me out of it."

"Thank God! But how'd you find Janine? I looked everywhere for her."

"I called her parents in Seattle. Janine didn't want to see you, but she had no problem seeing me. I left a message with her mother, and Janine called me back the same day. When I told her what we were doing, she signed on immediately. She still really cares about you."

Beth looked so happy and eager to please, I finally quit giving her a hard time. What I really wanted to know was *why?*

She pulled out a folded piece of paper from the pocket of her jeans. "This is only a copy. Peter has the original."

I recognized the messy handwriting as soon as I saw it. It was a letter from my mother to Peter, dated the week before she died.

"How come he never showed it to me?"

"He probably hoped he'd never have to."

As worried as I was about the letter's contents, it pleased me to see my mother's illegible writing once again.

Dear Peter—

Leaving you is one thing, but leaving Josh fills me with utter sadness and dread. He means the world to me, but let's face it, he's high maintenance. Kids like Josh need so much support and stimulation. I'm worried that after I'm gone, he'll look for his adrenaline rushes in destructive ways. I've worked hard at keeping his world full of excitement; his mind is his savior as well as his curse. Promise me if he starts to drift or sink, you'll drop everything you're doing to engage him. He's a good kid— the best—but it takes some work to keep him plugged in. There's no greater gift you can give me, Peter. I'll be watching over both of you always. P.S.—Josh loves Beth next door. Go to her first if you need help.

Beth grabbed the edges of my jacket. "Your mom thought you loved me—why'd she think that?" She inched closer until my back was against a giant pine. "Why'd she think that, Josh, huh?"

As I reached across the cool January night to kiss her, I changed my mind and turned away. "Mom knew I'd have a hard time without her? The queen of spontaneity actually planned this far ahead? She thought I was high maintenance?"

"You *are* high maintenance!" The romantic moment had shifted, and so did Beth. "Peter was so worried about those letters you wrote home from the road that he called me up one morning to brainstorm how to get you back on track. When you got home and neither of us could get you off the couch for months, he gave me the go-ahead to plan something. Let's face it, we all get caught up in games—my roommate hates me, my boyfriend's cheating on me, I'm having a spiritual crisis—I just thought a conscious game instead of an unconscious one might jolt you back to being yourself."

"So I guess those psych classes are paying off."

"Don't forget the drama classes. Got my money's worth on those too."

"You used to be such a terrible liar!" I said. "Kudos to your drama teacher."

"Don't you want to know about betagold?"

"That was my next question."

"I knew if she was in our little game it would raise the stakes, so I had the detective check her out. When she told me about betagold's charity work, Peter and I went back and forth before contacting her. As much as we hated to admit it, it seemed like she'd really changed. It was actually kind of fun working with her."

"I can't believe how much work you and Peter put into this."

"He paid for everything, and it cost a ton, believe me," Beth continued. "He was so worried about letting your mom down, it was really sweet."

I looked up to see Peter a few yards behind us. He was wearing a Dr. Seuss hat[117] and smoking a cigar.

"You did all this for me?" I asked.

---

[117] What was with all the wacky headgear? I was beginning to feel left out.

He nodded. "And for your mother. I didn't mean what I said about grabbing the ring off her finger and running. The years with her were the best times of my life."

"Don't you think therapy would've been cheaper?"

"Sure, but I felt I had to be a little more creative with you."

As insane and convoluted as Beth and Peter's plan was, I had to admire the effort and attention to detail. I didn't know what else to say besides thank you.

"I'm an events planner, after all," Peter said. "The question is, did it work? Do you feel alive again?"

"Sure, if you don't count the nightmares I had to go through to get there."

"A life-or-death situation will usually do that," Peter said.

"Reality can be painful," Beth added. "Of course so can fantasy, as evidenced by all the groaning you did about your kidney."

I was never, ever going to hear the end of that one. But there was a question I had to ask. "Was that part of the game, making me think Gus was my biological father?"

"No!" Peter said. "The woman playing the private investigator screwed up. Instead of reading from the fake Gus bio, she was looking at *your* file. We were furious with her."

"I nearly died when you came to Brown and told me," Beth said. "And God forbid you let go of the new story line. We all had to improvise."

"So my biological father is dead?"

Peter nodded. "After you started digging around, I hired a real P.I. to look into it. He died before you were born, just like your mother said."

I'd be lying if I said I didn't feel a pang of grief. Peter must've sensed it because he put his hand on my shoulder. "Sorry that mistake got your hopes up."

"It's okay," I said. "I'm used to paying the price of an over-active imagination."

"Speaking of paying, we owe the bank a bundle, but I've been working on that too. We shot footage to document your journey—Gus's brother-in-law, Joe, said you spotted him a few times with his videocamera. I'm flying to L.A. next week to pitch this to five different studios as a new reality show—contestants, prizes, audience participation as to the player's fate. Give my event-planning business a boost. What do you think?"

"You're kidding me, right?"

"I've edited all the footage into a great pilot. The thing looks amazing. You're going to be a star."

I looked over to Beth. "Please tell me this is part of the game."

She laughed. "Sorry."

"Hey," Peter said, "how about if I put you on as associate producer?"

I leaned against a maple and waited for them to tell me they were busting my chops. They weren't. The guy with the videocamera appeared from behind the bushes.

"Got all that, Joe?" Peter asked.

"Got it." Joe zoomed in for a close-up.

"So, Josh," Peter asked, "what did you learn?"

I stood there tongue-tied, watching Peter and Beth wait for me to say something profound. Instead, I just thought about how generous and crazy they were, and how much I loved them both. I thought about how life *was* a game, how I'd spent hours upon hours searching for the key to the universe, when all along, the door was already unlocked. I absorbed this new-found knowledge with a stupid grin on my face until the cam-eraman yelled "cut!"

"Do you remember when I gave you this?" Beth held up the wizard hat she'd worn at the "cast party" a few nights ago.

I told her of course I did; she'd given it to me at the first Larryfest in honor of the nickname she'd bestowed on me years before. I was finally inside the Victopian, which had served as command central for their operation. Peter was loading equipment into his car while Beth folded the various costumes and uniforms, some to return to the Brown theater department, others to donate to Goodwill.

"Out of all the things that are bothering me, the worst is that I never heard my mother's voice at Bloomingdale's that day. Those people were plants—my mother hasn't spoken to me yet."

"I guess that means you need to make a trip to Chestnut Hill before you leave for school. See for yourself if you can still hear her or not."

As if I hadn't planned on doing that already.

Beth cleared up several loose ends I'd been wondering about: They'd made their own Mass General and Princeton letterhead, a contractor friend of Beth's father had parked a backhoe and port-o-john at my favorite woods to make it appear as if construction was under way. The land mines were actually brake drums they'd gotten at an auto salvage yard.

"Why did I have to pay tuition and no one else did?"

"I figured the fake tuition would be a good way to start messing with your head."

When Beth answered the front door, I almost didn't recognize Gus. He wore pressed khakis, a button-down shirt and tie, and had reading glasses on a cord around his neck.

"Sorry to stop by unannounced. Just wanted to pick up my check."

Beth told Gus she'd get it from Peter and invited him in. I'd planned on making a fake vet appointment to get a chance to see him one last time. I welcomed the opportunity to talk.

"Doug Crimini, isn't it?" I extended my hand. "Nice to meet you." I asked about his job at the vet office.

"Been there seventeen years. Had a ton of vacation time saved up. Thought this whole thing sounded like fun." He had the same sparkle in his eyes he had while playing a spiritual leader. He pointed to the photo of Peter and me he'd noticed in my fake hospital room. "Seems to me your real father's been here all along."

I knew what he meant; Peter was no longer just the guy my mother married—he was my father.

"So you made up all the spiritual stuff?"

"At first I was just using notes from Beth, but you were so serious, I had to step up my game."

"The paint-by-numbers kits?"

He shrugged. "I got a whole case of them at Job Lot. I thought they might be amusing, and they were cheap."

190

I'd spent hours performing spiritual practice based on what Gus got on sale that looked *fun*? I had to let out a laugh.

"I have a guru too," Gus said. "I started applying several of his teachings to my role."

I asked him to tell me more.

"My guru is so evolved[118] he never complains, is always cheerful and kind, takes criticism without resentment, over-looks other people's mistakes, never lies, never is stressed, has no prejudice, never corrects people, understands when others don't have time for him, and is always grateful for every-thing he has."

I told him his guru sounded amazing. "Maybe I should study with him too."[119]

"Then get yourself a dog. They're a hundred times more evolved than we are."

Beth returned with a check and gave Gus a long hug. She told him if he ever wanted to sit in on any of her drama classes at Brown to give her a call.

He headed to the door then turned to me one last time. "What you think *does* manifest itself in the outside world. That wasn't just part of the game—it's true. Someone once wrote 'All paths lead nowhere, so it is important to choose a path that has heart.'"[120] He shook my hand. "And that's the last piece of advice I'm ever going to give anyone."

As I watched him walk to his truck, I realized I'd learned

---

[118] How evolved is he?

[119] Here we go again.

[120] I looked up the quote later; it comes from Carlos Castaneda.

more from someone *playing* the role of teacher than I'd ever learned from a real one.

"I owe you the rest of the chess pieces!" he called as he screeched his truck down the drive.

"You probably want to rest," Beth told me. "After all, you recently had surgery."[121]

I left her with stacks of clothes and pedaled over to Bloomie's.

I'd spent hours parsing out the various threads of Beth and Peter's plan. There were many loose ends, things I might not be able to wrap my head around for months. But something specific bothered me now. A scrap of conversation that stuck in my mind like the burr that attached itself to George de Mestral's pants.[122] I was also curious about my wireless connection with Mom. Maybe if I heard her again, she could give me some advice on my current problem.

"Nice party the other night," Marlene said. "But a little chilly. Those fur-lined tights my niece gave me really came in handy."[123]

Marlene told me Beth had contacted her months ago and had provided a few stock girls with exact dialogue to say when I finally arrived. Marlene had paged the girls to the department

---

[121] I told you she'd never let me hear the end of it, didn't I?

[122] An interesting story, actually. George de Mestral, a Swiss inventor and outdoor enthusiast, was fascinated by the burrs that stuck to his pants and dog during a hike. He examined the burr under a microscope and discovered how the hooks of the burr connected to the loops of his fabric. He played around until he came up with his own hook-and-loop system that he called Velcro—an acronym for velour crochet (French for velvet hook). But I digress. As usual.

[123] Too much information, thanks.

as soon as she saw me. Beth's intricate planning outshone even the most complex *Mission: Impossible* scenario. I left Marlene and cruised the different counters until I found a spot with good celestial reception.

"Mom, I read your letter. You were right—I did get derailed. But you married the right guy. He came through for me big time. Just the way you would have—dramatic, quirky, and fun. I'm okay now."

A salesperson with bright red talons gave me a shut-up-and-move-along look. I ignored her.

"Here's the thing, Mom. If I'm right, the game isn't over yet. I still think people are in danger." I stood in the middle of the department and waited for her response. I didn't have long to wait. A man carrying a dozen gift bags approached the counter closest to me. He was talking on his Bluetooth.

"You're right," he said. "Follow your instincts, but don't drag your feet."

I raised my fist in the air. Mom was back! I had one more stop to make before heading to the woods.

The light covering of snow seemed ominous instead of beautiful. I laid my bike on the ground and stood at the edge of the forest. I knew who'd be waiting close by.

"I can see your footprints in the snow!" I shouted. "I know you're behind those trees."

"Then come and get me," the voice called.

"You know why I can't," I said. "Unless I want to lose a limb in the process. Those land mines I saw were real. You had everybody fooled but me."

I kept my eyes on the trees as betagold emerged. She wore her camouflage tracksuit and beret.

"How did you know?" she asked.

I reminded her of her comment at Walden a few weeks ago. "You talked about antihandling devices. If the land mines in Gus's truck were fakes and the whole troupe knew it, why were you familiar with the intricacies of working with them? Only someone handling real land mines would know those kind of details."

"I handled the mines, all right. Three of them are right here in your precious hole."

"You've been trying to hurt me for years," I said, "but I never pictured you as the homicidal type."

She seemed taken aback. "Kill you? Why would I do that?" She wiped her nose with the tissue tucked inside her sleeve. "*I'm* the one jumping into the hole."

I inched closer and asked what she was talking about.

"Stop!" she shouted. "Any closer and I'll jump."

I stayed where I was.

"You want to know why?" she continued. "Because I'm old, because I'm tired. Because I'm alone."

I suddenly realized she wasn't wiping a runny nose but tears.

"Because the biggest enjoyment in my life is torturing a young man who wants to change the world. Pretty pathetic, don't you think?"

Was betagold being real, or was this just another part of the game? There was no way to know for sure; all I could do was be honest myself. "I thought I was donating my kidney to you—that should count for something."

"All that means is you're a better person than I am. One more reason to kill myself." She perched on the edge of the hole, arms and legs spread wide.

"What are you going to do, belly flop into a hole full of land mines? That's a horrible way to die."[124] I took another step as she wiped her eyes. "Where'd you get the land mines, by the way?"

---

[124] Even for betagold.

195

"There's a huge black market," betagold answered. "But you probably found that out in your research."

I inched forward a step. "I became quite the expert. Did you know there's a device you can bury near a mine that runs so hot, it burns out the explosives and detonator before they can trigger the mine?"

"You'd still have to find the mine to bury a device nearby."

"That, or you could attach them to the mines before they were buried." I lunged toward betagold and pulled her away from the hole. She wasn't bluffing; three mines stared up at me from the bottom. I reached into my pocket and took out the jerry-rigged remote I used every year to crisp Peter's turducken. "Those anti–land-mine devices reach 2,700 degrees. You can't ignite that kind of heat by hand." I aimed the remote at the first mine and clicked. A pop, then smoke rising from the ground.

"What did you do?" she demanded.

"I snuck into your room at Victopia last night and attached the anti–land-mine devices to all three mines. You're not the only expert in handling them."

When she tried to grab the remote, I lost my balance and almost fell into the hole. "Watch it!" I screamed.

She looked at me with such desperation, she could've been either a nominee for Best Actress or a woman in true despair. "Let me die," she said. "Please."

I told her I couldn't.

"You know what it's like to want to die. Don't you remember that kind of pain?"

As we stood on the precipice of the hole, I didn't think it

would be helpful to tell her that the only reason I'd ever entertained the idea of suicide was because she'd driven me to it. But this wasn't a fake suicide; it was real. Or was it?

"Please," she repeated. "Let me go."

Was betagold in serious anguish, or did Peter need a final scene for his reality show? Was she about to kill herself, or was Peter's cameraman filming from behind those oaks?

"It's freezing out here," I said. "Why don't we discuss this over coffee?"

She shook her head. "There's nothing else to talk about."

I'd learned something important early on from Doug the vet technician. I didn't have to buy into the 'us' and 'them'; I could choose to focus on the 'we.' I grabbed betagold's hand. "Okay. Let's do it."

When she looked up, it was as though she was seeing me for the first time. "You'd do this with me?"

"I was willing to die with you during a fake kidney transplant, and I'm willing to die with you now." I swung my arms, pulling hers alongside mine. "One . . . two . . ."

"Wait!" she shouted. "Are you sure?"

"About as sure as I'll ever be. Hurry up before I change my mind."

Her entire face broke into a huge smile. "Then let's go. One, two . . ."

Just as she was about to yell three, I let go of her hand and aimed the remote at the land mines. They both fizzled out before our eyes.

Betagold gazed down into the smoky hole. "So were you just playing with me?"

197

"I was wondering the same thing about you."

She took a long look around the woods. "It's pretty here. I can see why you like it." She wrapped her scarf around her throat and backed away from the hole.

"Take care of yourself," I said. "Maybe I'll see you around."

She stopped to take in the forest one more time. "Maybe. Maybe not."

I watched her walk toward the road, then carefully climbed down into my still-sacred space. I put on my gloves and cautiously cleared out the burned-out mines. I'd drop off the debris at the dump on my way home.

After this, Princeton was going to be a cakewalk.

Boston's South Station

Peter returned from L.A. triumphant. "They green-lit the show. We're going into production next month!"

As excited as I was for Peter's new career, the thought of my face being plastered across the nation's television screens was almost impossible to imagine. But when I began to complain, Peter stopped me.

"The studio decided to go in a different direction."

I asked him what he meant.

"You know those bozos in Lala-land. They feel they're not doing their jobs if they don't stick their noses in."

"What did they ask you to change?"

"Basically, you."

"That's great," Beth told me. "You didn't want to be on television anyway."

"Yes, but I wanted to reject them, not the other way around."

Peter elaborated only when I pressed him. "Okay, okay. They wanted someone a little less . . . nerdy."

"I'm not nerdy!"[125]

---

[125] Don't bother with your e-mails; I had to defend myself.

"Someone more, I don't know, athletic, photogenic, likable."

"Feel free to stop anytime."

"The good news is we're not in debt, you can attend school, and my events-planning career gets a giant bump."

I asked him how the series could possibly be a reality show if the studio reshot it after the fact.

"None of those shows are reality reality," Peter answered. "They're scripted, cast, and edited like every other show. After these past few months, you of all people should understand the shifting nature of reality."

He had me there. I told him to make sure and let me know when the show aired.[126] After much deliberation, I decided not to tell either of them about my incident with betagold yesterday. Peter would flip if he found out about her seppuku land-mine attempt; besides, I felt as if I'd wrapped up the confrontation nicely.

When Peter left the room to take a call, I used the opportunity to talk to Beth alone.

"All this effort you put out almost rivals our presidential campaign." I tucked a lock of her growing-out hair behind her ear. "That's a lot of work to go through for just a friend."

"You're not going to hit on me now, are you? Don't you think we both need time to process all this?"

I stared at the kitchen clock for a nanosecond. "There, done. Totally processed."

Beth punched me in the arm the way she always had, the way she hopefully always would. "Let's just wait and see, okay?"

---

[126] So I could plan on doing something else.

"What are we supposed to be waiting for?"

In an incredible combination of bad luck and timing, Janine chose that exact moment to knock on the front door. Beth put on her jacket and gave me a smile. "I guess we wait for another time." She kissed me on the cheek and let Janine in on her way out.

I didn't know who I was happier to see, Janine or Brady.[127] We made Caesar salads, then hung out in the basement.

"One thing you never told me," I said. "Since you weren't really studying with Gus in L.A., where were you while I was searching the country for you?"

"First I went back to Boulder, then I spent the winter in Costa Rica. Got pretty good at surfing. That's where I'm headed now."

So much for my next question.

"But I'm happy to visit you at Princeton after you settle in."

Question answered. "Do you think there's any chance of us ever being more than friends again?"[128]

"It meant a lot to me that you'd donate an organ to get me away from some manipulative jerk," she said. "It makes up for all the other stuff, for sure."

"So there's a chance?"

When she told me she didn't know, I rattled off a list of reasons why we were compatible. She listened thoughtfully but

---

[127] Of all the things you can call me, I'm happy to say dog-killer is no longer on the list.

[128] Don't hate me for hitting on Beth and Janine within five minutes of each other. I have feelings for both of them, okay? Besides, what good is altering your view of reality if you still can't get a girlfriend?

202

still didn't come around. "I love you, you're great[129] but you're kind of . . . high maintenance."

First my mom, then Janine? Was I *that* much more work to keep up with than the average guy?

"But you're still one of the most important people in my life," she said. "Let's see what happens."

We took turns on the swing for most of the afternoon before she had to go. I spent the rest of the night packing for school.[130]

"What do you mean I can't drive you?" Peter asked the next day. "You're going to deny me the parental privilege of taking my only son to college?"

I told him our parting scene at Princeton paled in comparison to the other adventures we'd shared these past few years. "Besides, you know what a junkie I am for public transportation. And I only have one bag." I didn't mention the fact that for the first time this year, I'd actually finished writing a sermon. The long train ride would give me ample time to crank out a few more.

Peter reluctantly drove me downtown to South Station. Thankfully, neither of us wanted a sentimental episode with violins and tears. Instead he bought me a veggie sub and a bottle of water, and instructed me to call when I arrived.

I found myself choking up when I finally had to say goodbye. But before I could say anything, Peter grabbed the sub from my hand. "Maybe I should go vegetarian too. Might be good to

---

[129] Here comes the worst word in the dictionary: *but.*

[130] Given the number of things I own, it took me about three minutes.

lose a few pounds before I start spending time in L.A." He took a giant bite of the sandwich. "People don't eat enough eggplant. It's such a great vegetable."

From a botany perspective, eggplant was a fruit, but I didn't want to squabble. Peter seemed as reluctant as I was to deal with the ramifications of this new separation.

"I'm not going to come home screwed up like last time," I said. "If that's what you're worried about."

"I'm not worried. Do I look worried?" He stopped chomping on the sandwich. "I'm petrified. Can we make a deal? Can we just have a normal year this year? Quiet, nose to the grindstone, nothing too unpredictable? I don't know how much energy I have left to keep up with you."

"*Me?* You're the one creating an alternate reality to get me off the couch!"

"I guess a little bit of you has rubbed off on me."

Still, I agreed to a calm and uneventful year. I took a bite of the sub to seal the deal. Peter gave me one last hug and told me he'd talk to me that evening.

When I tossed the sandwich wrapper in the trash, something on one of the café tables caught my eye. There were no empty coffee cups or napkins, just a hand-carved chess piece and a train ticket. I sat on one of the cane chairs and examined the piece—a maple pawn, beautifully carved. A pawn, often the first piece moved in a new game. The ticket was for a train leaving for Miami in ten minutes.

This chess piece has nothing to do with you, I thought. *Board the train to Penn Station and be on your way. Someone probably forgot this and is coming back for it. Mind your own business for once.* I asked the man at the next table if anyone had been sitting there; he said he hadn't seen anyone in that seat for the past hour. I brought the ticket to the information counter, but the clerk said he was going off duty and to put it back where I found it in case someone came looking. *This is just a coincidence,* I thought. But was it? Or could this possibly be the beginning of a new game? What awaited me—or anyone else—on the other end of this train ticket? I looked at the giant clock. Five minutes left for the train to Miami, twelve minutes to Penn. The two trains were departing on adjacent tracks. I ran to the platform, still unsure about which train to board.

I'd promised Peter this year would be simple and uncomplicated. On the other hand, the chess piece and train ticket appeared to be a sign. I stood at the top of the platform between the two trains.

I crossed my fingers and boarded.

Epilogue

"We live in a world ruled by fictions of every kind. . . . We live inside an enormous novel. For the writer in particular it is less and less necessary for him to invent the fictional content of his novel. The fiction is already there. The writer's task is to invent the reality."

J. G. BALLARD

"So are you going to tell me where you ended up?" I asked.

"Not really," Josh answered.

"Come on! That's not fair."

"To make a long story short—"

"I don't want the short story," I interrupted. "Give me the long version."

"Sorry, Janet. That's a different book."

As much as Josh's evasiveness infuriated me, I felt privileged to be walking with him through his wooded sanctuary. My son sat happily inside Josh's favorite hole, arms behind his head in full relax mode.

"Are you going to school?" I asked. "Moving home? What's next?"

Josh tossed my son a pinecone and smiled. "What are you now, my mother?"

I faked a laugh, although that's often how I felt.

Josh pointed to my son. "He looks pretty comfortable in there."

"You're sure you got all the land mines, right?"

"I think so." Josh couldn't contain his smile. "Are you going to help me out with the manuscript?"

I told him my editor had finally agreed to publish it, then asked him whom he wanted to dedicate the book to.

He threw another pinecone to my son. "Dedicate it to him," he said. "He reminds me of myself at that age."

"Don't even say that!" I said. "He's enough work as it is."

"What did my mom call me—high maintenance? She was probably right about that one."

"You think?"

He looked up at the sky and said he had to head back. He was the only person I knew besides my husband who could accurately tell time from the sun.

After I told Josh I'd call when the book was ready, he said he wasn't sure where he'd be but to leave a message with Peter. He thanked me for my help, said goodbye to both of us, and jumped onto his bike. I waved as he pedaled away.

Although I hate New England winters, I climbed into the hole with my son. It would be spring soon, but not soon enough for me.

"You said Josh's book was about reality. What does that mean?" my son asked.

"It means he's trying to understand the difference between what's real and what's not."

"Like this stick?"

"Real."

"And this leaf?"

"Real."

"And Josh's book?"

As a novelist, I spend a large part of my day in the fictional world; I wasn't sure I was the best person to answer my son's question. "Only Josh can tell you that. But I will say this—reality is totally overrated."

We sat in the deep woods, blanketed between the wind and the frozen earth. For some reason, I wasn't cold and stayed for almost an hour gazing up at the wild, open sky. I thought about the T-shirt Josh had worn under his jacket; he'd silk-screened the Gandhi quote "My life is my message" onto the pale blue cotton. As I stared at the clouds, I wondered what message *my* life conveyed. What kind of books did I want to write? What kind of person did I want to be? Was I moving through my days on autopilot or taking part in this messy, beautiful, chaotic world to the fullest extent possible? I questioned whether Josh had a better handle on his reality than I did.

It began snowing hard. I watched the large flakes swirl around us, ancient yet new. I stared as if I were inside a kaleidoscope observing the snow shift and dance. The flakes were ephemeral, and so were we—all we could do was enjoy the ride. But like Josh discovered, sometimes a situation called for action.

I climbed out of the hole and rolled a chunk of snow into a ball. I hurled the snowball at my son, who nailed my leg with one of his own. We raced deeper into the woods, the silence punctuated only by our laughter. I didn't feel cold or out of breath, just blissfully and fully awake.

GOFISH

JANET TASHJIAN

What did you want to be when you grew up?

Students ask me this all the time, and I wish I had a better answer. When I was young, I was too busy playing, reading, and studying to think about career goals. I envy people who knew what they wanted to be by age ten. I was not one of them.

When did you realize you wanted to be a writer?

Several years ago I traveled around the world, and when I got back to the States, I had to fill in some forms. One asked for my occupation and I put down "writer," even though I'd never done anything more than dabble. But deep down, I always felt being a writer would be the greatest job in the world. It took me several years after that to make that dream a reality.

What's your first childhood memory?

I remember cooking candies in a little pan on a toy stove that I got for Christmas. I was maybe three. I'm not sure if I remember it or if I just saw the photograph so often that I think I do.

SQUARE FISH

What's your most embarrassing childhood memory?
I was singing and dancing in a school assembly with my first-grade class when my shoe fell off. I kept going without the shoe, hopping around the stage—the show must go on.

What was your worst subject in school?
I always did well in school, but for some reason I forgot all my math skills and now can barely multiply. I'd love to know where all my math skills went.

What was your first job?
I've had dozens of jobs since I was sixteen—working on assembly lines, babysitting, washing dishes, waiting tables, delivering dental molds and telephone books, selling copy machines, working in a fabric store, painting houses . . . I could fill a whole page with how many jobs I've had.

How did you celebrate publishing your first book?
By inviting my tenth-grade English teacher to my first book signing. The photo of the two of us from that day sits on my writing desk.

Where do you write your books?
Usually in my office on my treadmill desk. But because I often write in longhand, I end up writing everywhere—on the beach, in a coffee shop, wherever I am.

When you finish a book, who reads it first?
Always my editor, Christy Ottaviano. We've been doing books together for almost two decades; I consider her one of my closest friends.

How do you usually feel once you've completed a manuscript? Are you ever sad when a book you are writing is over?
Relieved! I don't really miss my characters; they're always with me.

Are you a morning person or a night owl?
I like waking up early and getting right to work. I'm too fried by the end of the day to get anything substantial done.

What's your idea of the best meal ever?
Something healthy and fresh, with lots of friends sitting around and talking. Definitely a chocolate dessert.

Which do you like better, cats or dogs?
I love dogs and have always had one. I'm allergic to cats, so I stay away from them. They don't seem as fun as dogs, anyway.

What do you value most in your friends?
Dependability and a sense of humor. All my friends are pretty funny.

Where do you go for peace and quiet?
Like Larry, I head to the woods. I'm there all the time. I love the beach, too.

What makes you laugh out loud?
My son. He's by far the funniest person I know.

What's your favorite song?
Anything by Todd Rundgren, Joni Mitchell, Aimee Mann, Richard Thompson, or Elvis Costello. Geniuses, all of them. I also love U2's "Bad." I always have a list of songs in mind for

every book I write. I wish each book could come with a playlist. Music is a very important part of the writing process for me—I had so much fun writing *For What It's Worth*.

Who is your favorite fictional character?
As if I could choose just one!

What are you most afraid of?
I worry about all the normal mom things, like war, drunk drivers, and strange illnesses with no cures. I'm also afraid our culture is so invested in technology that we're veering away from basic things like nature. I worry about the implications down the road.

What time of the year do you like the best?
The summer, absolutely. I hate the cold.

What is your favorite TV show?
I love *Breaking Bad*, *True Detective*, and *House of Cards*. I watch a lot of British television, too.

If you were stranded on a desert island, who would you want for company?
My family.

If you could travel in time, where would you go?
To the future, to see how badly we've messed things up.

What's the best advice you have ever received about writing?
To do it as a daily practice, like running or meditation.

How do you react when you receive criticism?
My sales background and MFA workshops have left me with a very tough skin. If the feedback makes the book better, bring it on.

What do you want readers to remember about your books?
I want them to remember the characters as if they were old friends.

What would you do if you ever stopped writing?
Try to live my life without finding stories everywhere. For a job, I'd do some kind of design—anything from renovating houses to creating fabric.

What do you like best about yourself?
I am not afraid of work.

What is your worst habit?
I hate to exercise.

What do you consider to be your greatest accomplishment?
How great my son is.

What do you wish you could do better?
Write a perfect first draft.

What would your readers be most surprised to learn about you?
I litter McDonald's trash out of my car window when I drive—KIDDING!

What is your favorite sound?
My son laughing really hard.

What is your idea of fun?
Seeing comedy or music in a tiny club.

Is there anything you'd like to confess?
I love dark chocolate.

What would your friends say if we asked them about you?
She acts like a fifteen-year-old boy.

What's on your list of things to do right now?
EXERCISE!

What do you think about when you're bored?
Story ideas.

How do you spend a rainy day?
Watching comedy.

Can you share a little-known fact about yourself?
I love to make collages.

SQUARE FISH

The year 1971 is a big one for Quinn: the year he starts a band, the year he writes a music column for his school newspaper, the year he contacts dead rock stars on his Ouija board, and biggest of all . . . it's the year Quinn finally gets a girlfriend.

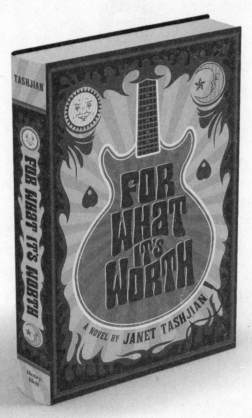

Keep reading for a sneak peek of

FOR WHAT IT'S WORTH

Rock and roll can change the world and save your life—and that's just for starters. I challenge anyone on the planet to remain in a bad mood when "Gimme Shelter" comes on the radio. It's physically impossible, right? Rock and roll can get you through a boring school year, give you something to bond over with your friends, even provide you with a reason to get out of bed in the morning.

You think I'm exaggerating? Listening to music is a critical step in growing up, as important as learning how to ride a bike with no hands. And not just rock and roll—pop, rhythm and blues, country, jazz—I don't care what it is, I'll listen to it. I'm like a junkie with a twenty-four-hour addiction, except the needle's not in my arm, it's on my turntable. Lucky for me, I live in the epicenter of the national music scene. Not just California, but Los Angeles. And not just Los Angeles, but Laurel Canyon. If you love music, there's nowhere else to be in 1971 but here. I can sit on my front steps, throw a rock in any direction, and hit someone making music for a living. Songwriters, drummers, singers, sound engineers—I've trick-or-treated at their houses since grade school. My sister, Soosie, housesits for Joni Mitchell, for crying out loud. Don't believe me? Ask Soosie to show you the scratches on her arm from Joni's cat—the singer/songwriter might be known for writing emotionally bare songs about her love life, but her feline companion is a lot less subtle with her claws.

Where do I fit into this musical melting pot? I'm the guy who chronicles EVERYTHING in his ever-present notebook—Elton John's first U.S. appearance at the Troubador, The Band's newest demo, any rock-and-roll tidbit a music freak like me might want to know about. I continually make lists of songs, artists, and albums—mostly when I should be doing homework. I begged my English teacher last year to let me write a column for the school paper about the music scene called "For What It's Worth," based on the Buffalo Springfield song. She finally relented, and I've been cranking out columns and lists ever since. Just to keep in practice, I stockpiled several of them this summer too. Speaking of Joni Mitchell, I just finished one about her dumping Graham Nash while she was on vacation. Women—they'll annihilate your heart every time.

The city is pulsing, the city is moving to an internal beat—*can you hear it?*

I can.

My sister, Soosie, just got her hands on my journal—WHICH WAS IN MY ROOM, WHICH I ASKED HER FIFTY MILLION TIMES TO STAY OUT OF—and threw herself on her waterbed in a fit of convulsive laughter. If I gave the false impression that I knew what it actually felt like to lose a girlfriend, I apologize. Truth be told, I technically don't know what it's like to have one, never mind lose her. Ow! (My bilious older sister now has me in a headlock, insisting I be even MORE honest.) Okay! Not only have I never had a girlfriend, I haven't yet found a way to cross the chasm between the witty repartee in my head and a conversation with a real live human female that lasts longer than two seconds. My number one goal for this school year is to have a relationship with a smart, funny, pretty girl I can talk to. Happy now, Soosie? Sheesh. Go away to college already.

FOR WHAT IT'S WORTH

8/71

After a particularly domestic
afternoon, Graham Nash wrote the song
"Our House" about the Lookout Mountain
home he shared with Joni Mitchell. The
album the song was on--Déjà vu--had
barely hit the airwaves when Mitchell
split for Greece without him. While
Nash was laying a new kitchen floor in
the home they shared, he received a
one-sentence telegram from Mitchell

informing him their relationship was over. Nash was crushed; he sat down at the same piano where he wrote "Our House" and wrote "Simple Man" about their breakup. It's almost as ironic as Joni writing "Woodstock"--the de facto anthem of the peace and love generation--from a Manhattan hotel room as she watched the coverage on TV.

While my parents are at work, I rummage through the garage until I find the long, curly brown wig Mom used to wear, then grab one of the scarves she sells in her store. I shut the door of my room and pull my Flying Burritos T-shirt over my head, exposing my bare chest, still tanned from the summer. I inspect myself in front of the mirror—neither my face nor chest has sprouted even the faintest hair. I adjust Mom's wig, tug my bell-bottoms a bit lower on my waist. But something's still missing for my spot-on Robert Plant impersonation, so I ignore Soosie's edict to stay out of her room—yes, I realize it's a double standard since I demand she keep out of mine—and grab a handful of silver bracelets from her bureau.

I stand in front of my turntable facing the toughest

decision of the day: "Dazed and Confused"? "Heart-breaker"? I decide to go with my old standby and crank up "Immigrant Song."

As Jimmy Page pounds out the opening riff, I jump around the room. *"A-ah-ahh-ah, ah-ah-ahh-ah!"* I stand in front of the mirror jangling the silver bangles on my arm and use the small piece of driftwood on my window-sill as a mic. *"To fight the horde, sing and cry: Valhalla, I am coming!"* I gyrate around the room, imagining thou-sands of fans singing along with me. It's as if one is actu-ally in the room because a flash suddenly goes off, blinding me for a second.

"Who are you supposed to be?" Soosie asks. "Wait! Robert Plant? That's hilarious!" She fans the Polaroid picture in her hands.

"Give it to me!" I whip the wig off my head.

"Not on your life." She runs into the bathroom and gets the book of matches Mom keeps near the vanilla candles. She holds a lit match over her head. "Encore! Encore!"

"Why do you always take the best moments and WRECK them? Can you major in RUINING THINGS at Brandeis? 'Cuz you'd get all A's." I remove the bracelets from my arm and throw them at her one by one.

I shove her out of my room, but she remains in the hallway, laughing. "I'm going to miss you, Quinn," she adds.

"That makes one of us."

I shove my desk chair under the doorknob so she can't come in—what I should've done before I started my personal concert. I slide the Ouija board out from under my bed. My aunt Tamara gave this to me for my ninth birthday, but I started using it regularly only a few months ago. Yet another CONFESSIONAL TIDBIT: I'm superstitious, a sucker for any kind of portal to the other side. So is my aunt, which is why she gave me this present in the first place. I know it's meant for two people, but sharing this sacred game with Soosie is unthinkable. I place my fingers gently on the planchette. (Yes, that's what the plastic disc is called; check the instructions inside the box if you don't believe me.)

"How will it be when Soosie leaves?" I ask.

Y-O-U W-I-L-L B-E F-R-E-E, the Ouija responds.

You're telling me.

Outside the room, Soosie gives a long series of knocks that get exponentially louder until I can't take it anymore and open the door. She's written "Quinn, 8/20/71" on the bottom of the photo. In it I'm all limbs and hair, a whirling dervish streaking across the room. "Come on," she says. "Help me cook my going-away dinner."

My sister knows me well enough to realize I can't stay mad for long when food is involved. While Mom will point out a bag of noodles for me to boil, Soosie makes zucchini muffins and carrot and ginger soup. Watching Soosie chop fresh tomatoes and cucumbers now, I wonder how she's going to handle living in a small dorm room outside of Boston.

"No fresh herbs growing on windowsills all year long," I say. "No olive trees in the backyard."

As a way of shutting me up, Soosie hands me a clump of parsley to wash while Carole King's *Tapestry* fills the kitchen. The album came out a few months ago and has been in serious rotation with not only Soosie and me but our parents too. Soosie babysat for Carole's girls many times and was even in the room when Carole posed on the windowseat with her needlepoint for the album cover.

I make one last attempt to get Soosie to leave her comprehensive album collection here.

"Why do you think Melanie and I are driving instead of flying?" she answers. "I've got eight milk crates full!"

Mom bursts into the room carrying a platter of deli meat and cheese. "Here I am! Let the party begin!"

Mom's food is almost always inferior to anything Soosie makes, but she seems so eager to please, I tear off the plastic wrap and make several ham and Swiss roll-ups to tide me over till dinner.

Soosie places a large bowl of tabbouleh on the kitchen table with crackers artfully arranged on the side. I've been so worried about missing her music collection that I almost forgot about meals. What will I eat after tomorrow? Is this literally the Last Supper?

As if she knows what I'm thinking, Soosie hands me a cracker loaded with tabbouleh and tells me she'll send care packages from Boston.

"It's supposed to be the other way around," Mom says. "But I do have some going-away presents."

She hurries to the porch and returns with a giant bag of clothes. Mom opened her shop with imported clothes from India, then started designing dresses and blouses on her own. It didn't take long before she was running the busiest boutique on the Strip. Soosie has always been voted best dressed in her class at school; me, not so much.

Soosie oohs and ahhs as my mother pulls out dress after dress from her bag. "This one's made from a vintage tablecloth," Mom says. "This blue one has doilies for sleeves."

"I think she also needs goodies for the road." My father holds open the back door with his hip while carrying a large cardboard box full of trail mix, fruit, and bottles of juice.

Soosie is beaming—a guest would think my sister's happy because of all the gifts, but I know better. Soosie's pleased because both my parents are home and the four of us are together, a real rarity.

Dad moves a stack of books and puts his boots up on

the table. He fixes cars at a high-end dealership in the Valley. After changing sparkplugs and overhauling engines all day, he usually retires to the garage to rebuild old radios and amps. He's much less gregarious than Mom, preferring to work with his hands than hobnob in the Canyon social scene. In all the years I've known him, I've never seen him without grease under his fingernails. He never talks about it, but he earned a Bronze Star for bravery when he fought in the Korean War.

The four of us spend the next few hours eating and telling stories until it's time for Soosie to pick up Melanie. We load the bags, albums, plants, food, and stereo into the back of her two-toned orange van—a trade-in from Dad's dealership that no one would buy so he fixed it up for Soosie.

"Call if you need *anything*, and I mean anything," Mom says in a blurry voice. I knew she shouldn't have opened that second bottle of wine.

"Change the world, make a difference, *contribute*," my father adds.

"Not too much pressure," I say.

Soosie rubs the top of my head the way she always has. "Come here, Mighty Quinn."

When she reaches over to give me a hug, she whispers in my ear. "I left you a present, but I'm not telling you where. By the time you find it, I'll be home for the holidays."

We wave goodbye until the van is out of sight. The sky teems with stars, and the air is filled with eucalyptus. It's the kind of Southern California night they write songs about. Here's the song I'd write tonight: *My sister's finally gone. Let my life and freedom begin!*